after
the
THUNDER
rolls away

...after Fate steps in

KAY LAYTON SISK

Dedication

For those who dare

Prologue

Rural Texas, June, early Saturday morning,
just past two a.m.

Adam Neely

Red and blue police lights spun in the star-filled night sky, casting eerie, split-second shadows on the two-lane highway and the girders of the narrow bridge. In the distance, the thwack-thwack of a helicopter grew louder. Police barricades closed the bridge on the far side and on this one, the one where Adam Neely sat sideways in the driver's seat of his late-model sedan, his right foot tapping on the asphalt and his head in his hands, the barricades held back people he knew but whose names his muddled mind couldn't now recall.

The sheriff's department and highway patrol were doing their best to send the onlookers on their way, to get them to back up and turn around and go home via the county road that added five miles to their trip back into town. Five miles to discuss what they hadn't seen while he sat here and adjusted to the new reality of what he had. He knew law enforcement were doing their best, just as the ambulance crews who had clambered down the

1

embankment thirty minutes earlier were doing their best as well. They *had* to be doing their best. Because if they weren't, then the friends--and people who had teenage sons and growing businesses quickly left the status of clients for an insurance agent--the friends he knew were in the car at the bottom of the river bank, those friends hadn't a prayer.

Adam felt his wife Sarah's touch on his right shoulder. She swiveled in the passenger seat and tried to hold him across the console. She was too heavy for that nonsense, for stretching her sixty-one-year-old grandmother's body to fit across a car seat, even if the doors were open, the summer breeze cooling his skin while the situation made him burn from the inside out. But Sarah needed comfort and he knew she didn't care what she looked like. She reached for him. The people in the car at the river were her friends, too.

Reluctantly, he pushed himself back into the car, lifting his left leg at the knee. He turned toward her. In the red and blue lights, the tears sliding down her cheeks resembled the tracks of a melting snow cone. "Are you sure it was them?" she asked again, as if he hadn't already answered that question when he'd limped up the embankment as she'd finished her cell phone call to 911.

"Honey," he started, sighed. "It has dealer tags. I have the photos on my digital in the back seat from when Mark brought it by this afternoon. How many new Jags do I insure each day?"

She nodded. "Those poor boys." She fidgeted some more, then opened the glove box and searched for her signature peppermint.

"We'll help all we can. Besides, you're just thinking the worst. They may not be dead."

But that was a lie. Better to have said, 'they may not all be dead.' The best he'd seen of the car before he stepped into a hole and wrenched his left ankle was the rear sticking skyward, the nose half in the slow-moving river, a tree under the carriage, the smell of gasoline just beginning to permeate the air. There was no movement in the car, and he had faced an awful choice: be stuck at the water's edge, unable to get back to Sarah and calm her, keep her away from the thing on the road, or climb out while he still had a handhold on the brush, climb out before his ankle swelled up and he was useless as a guide to the help that surely was on the way to them. And if Sarah hadn't found a cell signal... he couldn't let himself think of that. He had left the silent car with the smell of gasoline and the fates of two families tied inside and gone to Sarah.

The helicopter roared into view. Adam and Sarah looked out the windshield as the chopper hovered near the bridge. A tapping on the car roof broke the spell.

"Mr. Neely." The highway patrolman squatted inside the open driver's door. "Are you okay, sir? You weren't involved in this, correct?"

Adam shook his head. What an idiot he must appear, staring out the window as if he'd never seen a helicopter before, a vacuous look on his face if his matched Sarah's by half. A long night turned even longer and now this kid asking him... Adam took control of himself with a deep breath.

"I'm fine. Just twisted my ankle, like I said. We're just..." he looked at Sarah, at her glazed eyes, "we're just stunned."

The young man nodded. "We're going to bring them up now and transport them to Dallas as soon as the

3

chopper lands. I don't think there's anything else I need from you tonight. We'll be calling tomorrow to finish up. You can leave now. You know how to take the back road?"

Adam nodded as he watched the chopper, a red cross painted on its tail, set down as lightly as a dragonfly. Medics jumped off and met the ambulance crews. Two stretchers appeared.

"Officer..." Sarah broke Adam's reverie as she leaned over his back and snagged the young man as he was rising, "how many can be carried on that helicopter?"

Adam clenched his eyes against the answer.

"Two, ma'am."

"But there are four people in the car." Sarah's voice became a whisper.

"Yes, ma'am. There were four in the car."

Chapter 1

Eight hours earlier

Angel and Mark

"**H**ere, hon, hook me." Angel O'Shea took a step backwards toward her husband Mark. Her right hand clasped a pearl necklace together at the nape of her neck, while her left swept her freshly-colored hair to the side.

Mark sighed deeply and heaved himself off the side of their bed where he had been buffing his dress shoes. "You know," he grumbled as he took the clasp from her and squinted to see it, "I'd rather be at The Perch Pier than the country club winter dance. In the middle of summer. Ridiculous, Ange."

"Ice storm. Dance cancelled. Tickets already sold. Remembering any of this? Anyway, it's just June. And I chaired the committee. Which is why I was at the club all afternoon and why we have to go back early."

"But it's my birthday."

"Are you whining?" she asked. O'Sheas did not whine, or so they had always told the boys.

"Would it help if I did?" He laid the necklace on her neck and patted it.

5

He was whining. "Bad day at the store?"

"No. Good day at the store. Left by ten." He kissed her lightly on her bare shoulder, then pulled her to himself, wrapping his burly arms about her middle and squeezing as he nuzzled her neck. "I like the red in your hair." Another nuzzle, another kiss. "And you smell so good," he rubbed his clean-shaven chin on her shoulder, "let's just stay home and you can give me a personal birthday gift. Those old girls can run this party without you." He kissed her ear lobe.

Angel sighed as she pulled away and shook out her hair, the color of which he never mentioned unless it was to point out the encroaching gray. She leaned to the vanity mirror and checked the way the pearls laid on her neck. Hadn't she diffused this 'party on my birthday' situation two weeks ago when he'd put two and two together and realized the rescheduled dance--and the date wasn't her fault--was on his forty-sixth birthday? "Didn't I give you that birthday present last year? Aren't you always saying you want something different?" She put her flirtiest look in her eyes as she turned toward him where he'd resettled on the bed with a groan. "After twenty-five years, surely that one bores you."

"Twenty-six," he corrected. "You started giving me that present before we were married." He leered at her, the gleam in his blue eyes undiminished by time or the gray at his temples. If anything, it was intensified.

"You're a bad boy, Mark O'Shea." A bit more teasing and he'd be out of his grumpy mood. As if the man had anything to complain about.

"And I have a Jag to show for it."

Which just proved her point. He chuckled deep in his throat as he put the buffer back in the shoe kit he'd received as a high school graduation gift. It was the mark of the man that if something was still useful, he didn't discard it--and they had three storage buildings stuffed to the rafters to confirm it. "And Paulina doesn't have a clue."

That right there was enough to give him a happy birthday, so what was she worried about? Getting something over on Paulina Eubanks always brightened Mark.

"The games you two play. I don't know how you can be so sure she doesn't know. You told Eric, didn't you?" He ducked his head. Of course he told Eric. They'd probably been plotting this denouement for months. "Paulina has her ways to find out things."

Angel pulled the cobalt blue party dress from the hanger on the closet door. She'd bought it months ago to match her eyes. Now, looking at the flared skirt, she hoped she could get it on without the latest spandex accessory from the lingerie store. That's all she wanted to do: be squeezed into a twenty-first century girdle while she handed out canapés and danced with every old duffer in the place. For Mark's next birthday, come hell or high water, he was getting dance lessons.

Mark snorted. "I bought it out of town, I insured it this afternoon as Neely was closing, and I didn't drive down their street honking. Besides, Eric enjoys getting Paulina, too." He stood up and shook out his slacks, reached for his sports jacket on the wooden valet and fixed her with a look just as she started to shimmy into the dress. "I'll be downstairs when you're ready. Two hours early."

Angel rolled her eyes as she tugged the dress over her hips. She bit back the retort she always wanted to make, the one that started with how easy it was for a man to get dressed, especially when someone else did all his clothes, prepared his meals, and cleaned up after him. As always, it would serve no purpose, so she muttered it to herself as she heard the recliner in the den being propped up and the godawful latest example of techno-TV turned on. Good, he was content now and she could finish dressing in peace. Turning to the mirror, she spun for the dress to twirl about her knees and decided that if she didn't turn a profile to the dance floor while welcoming everyone, she could indeed go sans spandex.

The evening was looking up.

***

Marcus Denton O'Shea Jr. settled even more deeply into his favorite chair and scanned the array of remotes at his left elbow. How had it come to this, an assortment of electronics only their teenage son could efficiently use? And thinking of whom, where was William? Weren't they dumping him off at the Eubanks to spend the night with Ty while the four of them went to this charade? He selected a remote and pointed it at the TV in a vain attempt to turn down the volume. How gullible did Ange think he was? It was his birthday, ergo, it was a surprise party. How else had she convinced their friends to go so early?

But, he wondered as he tried another remote in order to get the desired effect, how were the boys getting out there? Who was bringing them? She wouldn't have the party without them, would she? And Jason and Travis, their older two, why hadn't they 'unexpectedly' shown up by now, just in time to put their mother in a well-rehearsed tailspin which she'd miraculously work out so they could all go to an event that supposedly had been sold out months ago.

Yeah, right. He wasn't born yesterday. Besides, had she suggested doing anything tomorrow night in lieu of tonight's celebration? No.

Should he practice his surprise face? Should he be shocked?

And where the hell was the remote with the volume control?

The back door slammed and the refrigerator opened, two things that didn't happen without each other, now that the elusive William had shown up. He was followed by Dweeb, aka Dwight Elbert on his pedigree papers, a golden retriever still in his puppyhood at age five. Angel had insisted on a female animal--"to even the odds"--but was lost to Dweeb the instant she saw him in the neighbor dog's litter.

"Dad!" He was breathless as he came running-- William didn't walk or saunter or even jog, William *ran*--to stand besides Mark's chair, a bottle of water shoved into his sagging front pants pocket and an ice cream bar half devoured, but whether by son or dog he hadn't a clue since Dweeb seemed to have ice cream on his nose. Oh, to be thirteen again and eat everything in sight. "Can't you turn that down?" the boy asked.

Mark shrugged and William, all lean long lines with hands and feet too pronounced for the rest of him but suggesting he'd fill out broadly as the O'Shea men were given to do, grabbed the first remote Mark had held and aimed it at the offending box. "Can't believe Mom's not been yelling down about that!" He flashed Mark a grin. And thank God he had straight teeth. He felt personally

9

responsible for the upgrade in lifestyle his first two sons had bought for the orthodontist. "But then you couldn't have heard her if she had."

He loved this last child, really he did. But, damn, he'd be glad when he was out of the nest. "Don't you need to get dressed?"

William looked down at himself. Ragged jeans, two tee shirts, both of which would have been rejected at the secondhand store, sandals. "Why? Just going over to Ty's."

Oh, she was clever, Mark thought. Have the kids change at the Eubanks'. Never let ol' Mark have a hint of suspicion. "Okay," he agreed. "Suit yourself."

"Well," the boy leaned down, one hand on the back of Mark's chair, the other too near his dress pants, "it would suit me to drive the Jag over. Can I?"

"Can or may?" Mark lifted the offending hand and gave it back to William. "Over where?"

"*May* I, cause I know I can. To Ty's. It's just five blocks."

He looked up at his son. "It's *your* birthday?"

"C'mon, Dad. That's not your birthday present. That's M-A-C, your middle-age crazy present to yourself." He emphasized each word. "Least that's what Mom says. I can't believe she let you get away with it." He crumpled the ice cream wrapper into a ball and tossed it into the air, catching it to throw it again. Dweeb barked and jumped. "I mean, what's Mom get out of this? *She's* not going to drive it."

Since when was William anyone's advocate, even his mother's? "Your mother gets anything she wants."

"Yeah, well, she's not going to *want* to drive it." Toss. Catch. Toss… "So can I? Travis let me drive his

Jeep at the Miller's farm."

"That is your brother's insurance, not mine." He caught the wrapper-ball on its next descent, disappointing dog and son alike. "Because I know I didn't hear you ask to drive my seventy-five thousand dollar dream car on the public streets. The one that, if your grades don't improve along with your ambition, the closest you'll get to, is polishing it."

"C'mon, Dad. Everybody else…"

Mark reared back, held his words, let his eyes speak for him. The only thing *everybody else* had better be doing in the O'Shea family was toeing the line.

"Then how about just let me pull it into their driveway?"

He quirked a brow.

"I could call Ty and tell him you have it and then he could tell his mother."

Mark cleared his throat.

"Or I could just be glad to be allowed to ride in the back seat."

"That's my boy." He tossed the wrapper back to him and pulled the recliner into its upright position. "Gather up your stuff, give Dweeb fresh water and put him outside." He stood and brushed at his sleeves. "I hear your mother coming."

Chapter 2

Seven and one-half hours earlier

Paulina and Eric

"**I** rushed home from the office, I bathed, I dressed, I'm out of breath, and you sit there in your work clothes. What is wrong with this picture?"

Eric Eubanks flicked off the bedroom TV and eyed his wife. Paulina, her shoulder-length brown hair swept back in a chignon, stood three feet from his lounge chair, the confines of her straight red skirt stretched to the limit as her bare feet were firmly planted shoulder-width apart. Her fists settled on her hips and her lips, never full and lush, disappeared in a straight line of disapproval. If she were chagrined now... "You don't have your shoes on," he chided.

"Eric Tyson Eubanks--"

It must have been a bad day for financial consultants.

He laughed and that, of course, made her madder, just as he knew it would. "Ah, sweetheart," he stood and started to circle her waist, but she side-stepped him, turning to toss Ruffles, the remaining half of semi-Persian cat siblings Ruffles and Ribbons, off the summer bedspread. Ol' Ribbons had had the good sense to shuffle off the Eubanks mortal coil a year ago, while Ruffles, age 12, hung on with a tenacity Eric had to admire. Either that, or this cat was more stubborn than even Paulina had figured, and she had actually chosen them.

"You are not bathed," she countered.

"That didn't use to bother you."

"Lots of things didn't use to bother me."

Amen. But he didn't say it aloud.

Her voice followed him into the master bath. "Why did you have to work with the crews today?"

"Miguel's mother fell and broke her hip and his wife has taken the kids to Corpus and Micky J's kid…"

"I get the idea." She leaned on the door jamb and twisted a gold and silver choker around her fingers. "But you knew we were going out and going out early."

"I also knew the job needed to be done." He rubbed his thumb and index finger together. "Client wrote that big ol' four-figure check, and I made out the deposit, put it right in the bank. That's the me-and-*you*-bank, Mrs. Eubanks." He skinned his dirt- and grass-stained tee shirt over his head.

"Let's just throw that one away."

"I wouldn't have any shirts if I did that every time you asked." He tossed it into the corner where he'd already pitched his socks and ragged jeans. "You'd have me working nude." He winked at her.

She rolled his eyes. "You are in a rare mood for someone about to stuff himself into a suit and make nice at the country club till the wee hours."

"It's Mark's birthday. Surely you haven't forgotten."

"As if Mark would ever let us forget his birthday." She fastened the choker about her neck, then jerked her head in the direction of the front windows, as Eric turned on the shower. "Oh, damn! Is that them already?" She spun and strode over to the blinds, peering through them. Eric craned his neck to watch from the relative safety of the bathroom door. "Oh, hell. It's somebody else. Who do we know that has a Jag?" She tapped her foot as she continued watching. "What is Mark O'Shea, that cheapskate, doing in a new Jag?" She whirled to Eric just as he ducked back into the bathroom. "Did you know about this?"

"Can't hear you over the shower!"

Ty's running footsteps reverberated along the hallway wooden floors and then through the walls, bouncing into their bedroom along with the boy. "Mo-om!" he was shouting as Eric stepped into the shower, "Guess what?"

"Just a minute, darling," she called from just outside Eric's watery isolation booth.

He tried on his best sheepish look as Paulina flung open the shower door. "You owe me!" She slammed it shut.

As if he ever hadn't.

***

She had been set up.

Paulina wasn't about to give Mark the satisfaction of running to see his newest acquisition. "Go see if you can get a ride around the block, Ty. Tell them we'll be there in a minute."

The bedroom door slammed in her only child's wake. How had Angel ever managed three?

Well, she hadn't worked, that's how, unless one counted the couple years she'd helped get Mark's business started, then another as it expanded. But since then 'volunteer' was the word most often attached to Angel O'Shea's name. Fund-raiser. Committee chair. Honoree.

Thank God she had a profession, Paulina thought, as she slipped on stiletto sandals and checked her makeup once more. Thank God she wasn't just a housewife.

Angel met her on the front porch. "Prepare yourself to be impressed," she murmured out of the side of her mouth.

"Oh, I'm impressed all right. Impressed Mark would turn loose that kind of money."

Angel laughed. "I can hardly wait to hear his father's opinion on it."

"And what's your opinion?"

"Good question." Angel spun on her heel and faced the three males with their heads in the trunk. "Cheaper than a mistress." She paused. "I think."

Paulina let the comment slide. "Isn't that the wrong end to be admiring?"

"GPS? Stereo system? Speakers? Measuring for golf clubs?"

"When you were a kid, Mark," Paulina started as she stepped down from the porch and onto the circular drive, "one inspected under the hood." She stood at the driver's door and waited for him to come to her.

"When I was a kid, Pauli," and he had the nerve to grin when he called her that, "I thought a Jaguar was a cat."

"Well, then, you've increased your vocabulary." She didn't want to admire the dark green vehicle, but couldn't help herself. "What do we call this color? Money ill-spent?"

He grinned and chuckled. "We call it the color of

15

envy."

"Oh, I'm not envious, Mark." She ran her hand lightly over the door frame and stooped to appreciate the leather before sitting in the driver's seat. "A bit covetous maybe, but never envious. I don't suppose I get to drive this wonder?"

"Pauli," he was expansive as he came to stand beside her. "Not on your life."

"Humph!" She twisted herself into the driver's seat and put her hands on the steering wheel. Nice, nice, nice. "Before the night is over, you'll need me to drive you home. I know you, Mark." She quirked a brow at him and timed the rest of her response. "Beer, beer, beer."

"It's my birthday. I'm going the single-malt route."

"Is this your birthday?"

"You two wear me out," Angel laughed as she leaned a hand on the hood. "Where's Eric?"

"Dressing. Had to work with the crews today. Why, I don't know." She ran her hands over the steering wheel. "Look, you've got a phone in the steering wheel. No excuses not to call home now."

"He works with the crews so you can eat." Mark reached over her. "I had a hard enough time keeping William's hands off everything. I think you're worse." He pulled on her wrists and made her get out of the car. She winked at Angel as she let him tug her out.

"You're who's worse--worse than an old maid with a new boyfriend." Paulina dusted her hands as if she'd encountered dirt in the pristine car. "I'll go check on the boss man."

Her heels tapped on the concrete drive and up the steps. The front door opened as she got to it. Eric came through, navy blazer swung over his shoulder, hair still damp. "Mark," he called as he cleared the steps with a bound, "did you get a new car?"

"For Chrissake," Paulina muttered to herself between her teeth, "do they never grow up?"

Chapter 3

Four hours earlier

Mark and Angel and Eric and Paulina

It was not a surprise party.

Mark sipped his expensive single-malt and licked his lips to enjoy every drop. The whisky at home was calling to him. For the bar tab he was running up, he could buy a bottle at the store--and he'd leave to do just that except Angel had cleverly tied him here by making him their transport. Not that he'd be driving home. No, Paulina had nailed him on that one. She didn't drink and was always the designated driver. Most of the time, it was a relief. Tonight... well, tonight, he wished he could drive home.

Now.

Not that the party was bad. Far from it. Everyone else except his fellow cohorts at the bar was into the spirit of it. The winter decorations were up and he had to admit the place did feel cooler looking at snowflakes and ski slopes, than at beach balls and a cheerful sun. Angel had done a great job on the welcome, had everybody laughing. She'd gone too far in suggesting they do it every year, but the good ol' girls would disavow her of that notion soon enough, so he needn't worry.

So where was the belle of the ball? He craned his neck to look through the bar's double French doors and found her being led around the dance floor by Edward Grimes, stuffed-shirt and expert on everything. She looked miserable but that fake smile was plastered on her face. He'd rescue her, but he had a Scotch to finish. Besides, he didn't like to dance, felt like a lumbering ox. She got him on the dance floor once a year, and despite the snowflakes on the walls, tonight wasn't New Year's.

"She'll be disappointed if you don't at least *ask*."

Mark looked over his shoulder. Paulina.

"Ask what?"

"Really, Mark. Don't be obtuse." She turned to the bar, rattled a nearly full tea glass at the bartender. "Standifer, I'm desperate for limes and they've run out on the wussie's drink table." She obligingly held her glass out for him and he plopped two tiny lime halves on top of the ice. She shot him a smile. The old man blushed and turned away.

"How do you do that--charm the pants off that old man? There ought to be a law. He's old enough to be your father." They both turned to watch the action in the other room.

"Prosecuted him on a public intoxication charge when I was first starting out." She sipped her tea and rested her elbows on the bar. "That got him into rehab and sober. But you know that. You just like to ask and make me remember what I used to do."

Mark rolled his eyes, ignored her last comments. "And he's a bartender?" He slid a glance over his shoulder at the man.

"Who better to know when *you've* had enough?" She

19

shook her head back and held her hand out. "Key."

"You want it already?"

"It's all about power, Mark. You know that." She twitched her fingers.

He dug into his pants pocket and dangled the single key above her open palm. "Say please."

"Say up yours."

"Is that what they taught you in law school?"

She simpered a smile and he laid it in her hand. "You cannot keep it at your house overnight."

"Why? You planning to sleep in it?" She rubbed her fingers over the key before curling her hand about it.

"Well, twinkle-toes there will be dead to the world. I might as well." He watched Angel be led back on the dance floor by Eric. "Looks like your other half will be worn out, too."

"He's always worn out." She puckered her lips, sucked on her cheeks. "I think he was born worn out."

Mark chuckled. "You're in a rare mood, Pauli."

"Just living up to my reputation." She pushed herself to stand straight and absent-mindedly deposited the key into her cleavage. Blowing him a kiss, she sash-shayed out of the bar.

Sweet Jesus, what a piece of work! Mark shuddered and pushed his now-empty glass in Standifer's direction. The barman cocked an eyebrow. "Better make it club soda. I've got to be sober enough to tell her how to put it in gear."

Standifer humphed. "Miz Eubanks already got that figured out." And he winked.

Yeah, Miz Eubanks thought she had everything figured out. Mark pushed himself to stand and went to find the dessert table.

***

"Wonderful party. You're a hit. They'll be all over you to do it again next year." Eric squeezed Angel's side, then spun her away in a swing dance move guaranteed to be felt in the morning by both of them. She caught on the end of his fingers and spun herself back.

"Over my dead body."

"Over Mark's. Noticed him in the bar with his bottom lip on the ground."

"Maybe Paulina'll tell him to be careful or he'll step on it."

Eric laughed and his blue eyes twinkled. "Nah, she'll step on it for him." He spun her again, his six foot frame stretching to reel her in.

"You've got to quit that. Ed Grimes trounced on my feet so much I'm going to wear steel-toes next time." And she was out of breath. Would the spandex have helped?

"Then let's get something to drink." He abruptly pulled her from the floor and headed to the punch bowl, dragging her in his wake.

Angel accepted more congratulations as she sipped her un-spiked brew. Smile, smile, smile. Tell everybody, no, can't do it again. Sequels are never as great as originals. Look for Mark.

He was usually the life of the party, cementing a spot in front of the punch bowl if it were spiked, or out on the putting green if there was enough interest to drag the men out that way. Tonight he sulked in the bar.

"Eric--" she caught him pulling a rose from the centerpiece and fashioning a boutonniere for himself.

"You need to let me make the floral contacts next

time, Angel." He studied the flower, grimacing. "I might even get some flowers from private sources."

"That's sweet, Eric." But not what she wanted to discuss. The flowers looked fine; he was being professionally picky. "Mark thought this was a surprise party for him."

"Yeah, I know." He was preoccupied with pulling three white rosebuds and weaving their stems. If the party weren't more than half over, she'd scold.

"So does he suspect about tomorrow?"

"Not a clue." He held up his creation and reached for her hair. She didn't fight him, just let him tuck the buds around the side clip. And knowing Eric, she looked twice as good as she had when she left the house. "But you'll have to put up with the sulk." He was pulling red roses.

"Eric, go demolish another bouquet."

"Have you seen Paulina?"

"She was in the bar…" she scanned the area "…but not now. Maybe the ladies'."

"Will it look strange if I camp outside of it?"

"Nothing you do is strange. Everyone just chalks it up to an artistic soul."

"An unfulfilled artistic soul."

"You've been listening to your wife too much."

"You don't think I'm unfulfilled?"

"I think you've had too much to drink."

"Prob'ly." He winked and sauntered off in the direction of the restrooms, making an abrupt right turn onto the patio. Angel caught the red of Paulina's skirt just outside the doors.

She sought out her husband. Not in the bar. Not with Paulina because now she could take a step and crane her neck and see the packed patio. Not holding down their table. Ah, the cheesecake bar. Just exchanging one vice for another. And he didn't need the calories either. No matter how much he exercised, Mark O'Shea was a big man... and at 46, a slightly overweight one, now surrounding his sorrows with a sugar high.

Come tomorrow night, when the boys "unexpectedly" showed up along with half the neighborhood, their parents, and the stores' employees and spouses, then he'd be so busy taking the birthday good wishes, he wouldn't have the time to eat.

Ed Grimes caught her eye and she smiled wanly, turned and found sanctuary behind the door marked La-Tees.

***

Judge Hanson. The last person Paulina wanted to engage in conversation this evening raised his glass to her as she entered the patio. The dirty old man. Who did he think he was? Granted, attorneys were supposed to get an extra layer of thick skin upon graduation, but that old man had put her in "her place" once too often during her career, and she still bore the scars, was *not* dealing with him for society's sake. She spun on her heel and into her husband's arms.

"Sweethearts for a sweetheart." Now Eric was holding a sprig of baby's breath and red roses out to her and, if her guess was correct, about to do something to her hair she would not like.

Judge Hanson wasn't looking so bad.

"Eric, what *are* you doing?"

"Finishing your coiffure."

She sighed, stood still. No sense in starting a public display. She'd let him get it out of his system and be glad it was roses and not another drink in his hands. What was with the men tonight? Mark had an excuse, although it was one he would regret tomorrow. She smiled at the thought.

"I knew you'd like it." Eric kissed her on the cheek. "Oh, look, Judge Hanson wants your attention."

"That's not all he wants, Eric." She patted her husband's chest. "Let's dance."

He reared back. "You really are in avoidance mode." But he took her hand, shot a loud comment over her shoulder to someone she couldn't identify. "Pauli's hot for my bod on the dance floor." A laugh and they were joining the other couples halfway through a slow number.

"I wish you hadn't done that."

"Loosen up, Paulina." He hugged her closer. "C'mon, let's fool them all and let 'em think we're still in love."

"Oh, Eric." Tears shot to her eyes. How could he? How could he doubt her? "I do love you."

"I know, sweetheart." He dipped her over his left arm at the end of the number. "You're just not still in love with me."

***

Eric wasn't quite sure what made him say it, what made him accuse her. There was no evidence, no hints, no hot trail. But he knew. Didn't even know if there was someone else, just that there was no longer him. He'd known for a long time. He hadn't slept next to this woman for over twenty years without knowing the 'in' had left 'love' a long time ago.

He pulled her upright. She smoothed her skirt, blinked her eyes. A tear slithered down her cheek and she

24

grabbed his coordinated hankie from his breast pocket and brushed it across her face. "Damn, it's hot in here." She said it just loudly enough to draw a sympathetic murmur from Sarah Neely who was sweating profusely, even for an middle-aged, overweight gal. "Race you to the john," Sarah said and Paulina obligingly followed in her wake.

Well, he was screwed now. He'd like to blame it on the alcohol, but he hadn't had a beer in an hour and then he'd only had three--or was it four?--all evening. Where was Mark? He needed an ally.

And perhaps a place to spend the night.

He shook his head in disgust with himself. How had he gone from fashioning flowers for her hair to kicking himself in the balls?

Well, dammit, it *was* the truth. Did she stay for convenience sake? Hell, Pauli had never done a convenient thing in her life. Could the solution be as simple as a vacation away, just the two of them? They'd already booked Cancun with Mark and Angel so more time off was impossible this season. In summer, a landscaper has to be everywhere all at once. Just like in spring and fall. Now, winter... Might the Eubanks have survived until winter if he hadn't opened his big mouth? He wasn't so sure.

Where was Mark?

As if he felt the vibes, his friend appeared at his elbow holding out a plate of cheesecake slices, a fork stuck like a shovel in the middle piece. "Here, sober up. Pauli looked like she was about to fry you."

With friends like this... Eric took the cake plate. "I am sober." He speared a cherry and put it in his mouth. "More's the pity."

"The girls aren't happy with me either. Angel's convinced I'm a sot at heart and Paulina thinks I'm a cad."

Eric was silent as he started on the chocolate.

"This is where you're supposed to defend me."

"A sot and a cad. I was just thinking it was appropriate." He smirked just as Mark's eyes narrowed. "It's your birthday. Be what you want to be." He finished with the plate and set it on the closest dirty dish tray. He dusted his hands. "Since my wife won't dance with me again and yours is in charge of clean-up, let me buy you a birthday drink." He swooped his hands toward the bar. "Lead the way."

"Now you're talking."

Chapter 4

Two and one half hours earlier

Angel and Mark

Midnight. The hours for this party had been clearly stated: 8 until midnight. The committee had even spelled it out. Only New Year's at the club had so many people here at 11:30. Why couldn't they all go home?

Angel knew she should be happy: the surest sign of a bad party was everyone beating a hasty retreat to the front door with two hours remaining. God knows she'd been on both ends of those. But a full house thirty minutes before the official end? *Give me a break*, she thought. They'd still be cleaning up at one.

Well, it was her own damn fault. If she hadn't decided on a surprise party for Mark tomorrow... She'd just get through it and collapse on Sunday. She'd done it often enough before.

Her eyes roamed over the room. The food was gone. The punch had turned non-alcoholic at eleven, but she'd wager half the people dipping into the sweet concoction thought they were still being lifted high. If Standifer would stop serving in fifteen minutes like he promised, then they'd just hand a broom to everyone still there at 12:05. Perfect! She smiled to herself. Absolutely perfect.

And the first two brooms were going to Mark and Eric, holding down one end of the bar and nursing beers. Someone was going to have an hellacious headache for his party tomorrow. How could Eric let him do it?

How could she? That was easy. If he was a big enough boy for a shiny new Jaguar, he was a big enough boy to watch his intake. Besides, she thought as she entered the bar and tapped him on the shoulder, he still hadn't danced with her.

"Wonderful party, honey." He didn't miss a beat as he turned to her. "When can we go home?"

"When you dance with me and we get the majority of the cleaning done so the staff won't be so overwhelmed tomorrow."

"Nobody else cleans their parties up, Angel. Just you," Eric interjected as he leaned around Mark.

"That's why I'm special." No one faulted Angel O'Shea for shirking, not even at the club.

"You're always special to me." Mark looped an arm about her waist and pulled her to him. "Why can't I just sit here?" He quirked a brow. "It's my birthday."

If she heard that once more… "Last time I am ever planning an event on your birthday." It was all she could do not to grit her teeth.

"Good!" He emphasized it with a squeeze.

She pulled out of his embrace and turned to go. Paulina waited at the bar doors, a cup of punch in her hand. "Standifer," she announced as she walked in, "let's jazz this up." She stared past Angel to Eric and hairs prickled on the back of Angel's neck, prickles which had nothing to do with the summer temperature. Since when did Paulina jazz anything up? Standifer's eyes had widened. She shook the glass at him. "I need three limes." She turned a cat-grin to her husband. "And a cherry."

Time to find the brooms.

"Now, you're sure that's all, Angel honey? There's not one more cobweb to be swept?"

Mark stood on the top step to the club's cut glass entry doors and spread his hands wide. Yes, he was being a bit of an ass. All right, he was being a big ass, but by God, if she volunteered to chair one more thing and then decided to clean it up... or decided he could, he was going to put his foot down. He had not worked so hard all these years just to see his wife be the cleaning staff.

She turned to him, the blue skirt swishing about her legs, catching the light from the parking lot, shimmering as it fell about her calves. She put a fist atop her right hip and set her mouth. Her foot tapped and Mark knew his wife had had about all she was going to take from him. Thank goodness only Eric was around, Paulina having gone to get the car. But then they were none too happy with each other either. Well, wasn't this going to be a pleasant trip back into town? He heard the club doors open behind him, but he didn't dare look over his shoulder.

"Angel," Adam Neely called, "Sarah wants to know if you saw her shoes. She kicked them to help clean and now she insists on finding them. I told her we'd come look tomorrow, that I'd bring the car right to the edge of the steps, but no..."

"They're in the kitchen," Mark answered for Angel, but he didn't take his eyes off her, "if they're white." He paused and his only excuse could be that the devil made him do it. "I saw them when I put my broom away."

The left hand fisted on the other hip.

"Thanks," Adam called, "y'all have a safe trip home. See you at ten for golf." The doors swooshed in his wake.

Mark gave her a limp smile.

"I know where you came from and you're the last person to be too proud."

"Pride has got nothing to do with this, Ange." Not really, did it? "I'm tired. It's one and we're teeing off at ten. You heard Adam. It's the men's association."

"That is so far from the truth. You're just upset because this party wasn't all about you." The roar of the Jaguar engine hid the rest of her comment. She turned to the front passenger door but Eric jumped in front of her, opened the back.

"C'mon, Angel, sit with me. We'll let the sourpusses have control from the front."

He winked at Mark as Angel disappeared into the back seat, scooted over.

Thank God for friends, Mark thought, as he hopped in the front with Paulina. "You did bring your license, didn't you?" he asked as she popped it into Drive and they left the club behind.

Fate's First Decision
Angel and Eric

Prologue
Highway patrolman Greg Glass

Being first on the scene, especially to a highway incident called in by a frantic woman, was a good news/bad news proposition to Patrolman Greg Glass's way of thinking. The first guy got to handle the situation and, if he did it well, impress his superiors when it came time for review. The first responder confirmed the need for the second ones, the ambulances and fire trucks. God forbid, a mercy helicopter.

But the bad news, when bad, was filled with terror. People on the brink of death, witnesses too upset to be of any help. The bad news had him in chaos-management and it really wasn't his forte.

Greg Glass hadn't found chaos at the scene on the two-lane highway that lead back into town from the exclusive country club he'd never be able to join. No, he'd found a woman sobbing in the front seat of her car, a man dragging an opened blanket across the highway to cover an object in the road. He was limping and grimacing and sweating with the effort, all clearly outlined in the headlights from Greg's cruiser.

The dispatcher hadn't mentioned a body in the road.

"Sir!" Greg called to the man and he stopped laying the blanket to look up at him. His eyes were glazed. What had the dispatcher said the name was? Greg cursed that he never paid enough attention. "Mr. Neely?"

The man nodded. "There." He pointed his chin over his shoulder to where the guardrail was broken and the new-growth trees smashed through. The headlights of the Cadillac marked the path. "They're through there." He went back to covering.

"Mr. Neely." Greg stepped in and took the blanket edge, cast a quick peek under it. Shoo... a deer. Thank God, just a deer.

"I can't tell if she's still alive or not. I was never much of a hunter." The man shook his head slowly and pulled the blanket from Greg's fingertips, returning it to cover the doe, which was, mercifully, dead. He turned back to his car. "My wife." He limped to her.

"Are you hurt, Mr. Neely?" Greg followed the man.

"I'm okay. But my friends, they're down there. I'd go with you, but..."

Greg flicked on his flashlight as he left Neely resting against the hood of his car. He carefully lifted his feet over the damaged rails, controlled his skid as he scrambled down the embankment. He followed the tire marks and the faint smell of gasoline, but the vehicle wasn't hard to find.

A new Jag. God, what a waste! Its rear rested on a larger tree, and the front lights were buried in the river's edge. He shone his light about the interior. Peering around the now-deflated airbags, he saw two couples. *My friends*, Neely had said. A man and a woman in front and back. His light traced the faces, doubled back on the man in the front passenger seat. Mark O'Shea. Hell, he'd been in Mark's store just last weekend. God, no.

The driver. Not Mrs. O'Shea. Paulina Eubanks. He'd heard stories about her days in court.

Which left their spouses in the back seat.

There was no movement from inside and he'd wager from the tilt of former Assistant DA Eubanks' head that her neck was broken. Her husband in the back seat moaned and Greg gave a silent prayer of thanks as he heard the first ambulance siren.

This, this was the waste.

Chapter 5

Monday, three days after the accident

The alarm was too loud, too long, too... too wrong. Since when did Mark set his alarm rather than relying on hers?

And he was all over her. Her arms wouldn't move, she couldn't breathe, her legs were asleep, her head was under the pillow.

Angel fought to awaken, to get out from under Mark and over to the clock which was making all that racket. She pulled and twisted, but her eyes wouldn't open. There was someone whispering her name.

"Angel, Angel, shhh, shhh, honey."

A woman's voice. Familiar but not supposed to be in her bedroom.

"Calm down. It's going to be okay." There were hands on her shoulders, hands holding her in place, breath on her face, the overpowering smell of peppermint. "Angel, open your eyes. Please, Angel. It's okay. It's all right."

Like calming a hurt child.

Slowly, she followed the instructions, stopped trying to lift her arms, to twist her legs. That wasn't getting her anywhere. She cracked her eyes. Everything was blurry. She shut them again.

"No, Angel, stay with me. Open your eyes." Her shoulders were shaken gently.

Mark was still on top of her. Or was it this woman? This just didn't make sense. Why couldn't she breathe right? But if she opened her eyes maybe it would clear up.

Angel willed herself to be still, willed her breathing to be regular. She'd done this three times for the boys' births, three sets of Lamaze exercises, three successful natural births with no drugs, only breathing, focusing. She could focus.

She eased her eyes open. What was Sarah Neely doing in her bed?

"Sarah?"

"Good, you know me." Sarah was frantically searching her eyes, then, "Oh, I need to call," and she leaned over Angel and grabbed something, pressed it.

"Sarah, what are you doing here?"

"Oh, I know, it should be your mother or your sisters, but they are absolutely exhausted. I made your dad take your mother to the cafeteria and then to sit outside and get some air. And Mark's folks… well…" Sarah's voice trailed off as she let go of Angel's shoulders and straightened up, relieving some of the pressure on her body.

Angel tried to form a question. Mark's folks? Mark didn't have *folks*. Mark had combatants. This didn't make sense.

She struggled again to sit up, but Sarah eased her back. "Now, just be calm. Be still. The nurse is coming."

"What nurse?" Angel's eyes darted about the room.

Blue-gray walls. Red roses in a vase by the window. Shadows cast by the blinds. A TV hanging in the air. More flowers, daisies and something purple. Rails on her bed. "Where am I?" Except Sarah had responded to her, she'd think she were dead, in her casket, surrounded by funeral sprays. Or perhaps she was dead and Sarah was lodged in her imagination, one of the last people she'd talked to on the other side.

"Oh, dear." Sarah wet her lips and twisted her hands. "You're... ah... what do you remember?" She crunched the peppermint in her mouth.

"That you're not supposed to be in my bedroom."

"Well, Angel..."

"But we're not there, are we? Can you," God, her head was pounding, "can you cut that damn alarm off?"

"There's no alarm, honey. It's the monitors. Your heartbeat. You know, everything."

Now Sarah bit her lower lip.

"Where's Mark?"

The door opened, a whoosh of air against metal, heavy footsteps, a flurry of excitement from outside. She turned to the noise. "Mark?"

A strange woman in a lollipop-decorated shirt and lime green pants was headed right for her. An ID-badge, a stethoscope. Scrubs. The modern nurse's uniform. But why was she *here*?

"Where's Mark?"

"Angel, just ease back." Gentle, but quite firm, hands pushed her back to the bed. "Thank you," the nurse said to Sarah, dismissing her in a polite, but off-hand, way. She already had a flashlight in hand and was pulling on Angel's eyelids. The light hurt. Angel squirmed.

"We love you, baby," Sarah said, her voice choking.

She kissed her fingertips and laid them in the vicinity of Angel's feet, then left.

"Where's Mark?" she demanded again after the lights were gone. She blinked to clear her vision.

"Angel, what do you remember?"

"What am I supposed to remember?" Perhaps a different tactic was called for. "Where are my children?"

"Here, Mom." There was a lot of commotion at the door and she jerked herself from the nurse's hands, twisted, lifting her left arm with the tubes and needles in the direction of Jason's voice. He was through the door, Travis in his wake, both of them pushing William back.

"You can't come in," Travis told him and a string of expletives reminiscent of Mark fouled the air.

"Why can't he?" she asked. Why were there needles attached to her? She stared at them, seeing them for the first time, the realization that something was terribly, terribly wrong sending chills down her spine. The facts were in front of her and still she couldn't quite connect the dots.

"Just what I was asking." William pushed past his older brothers and knelt beside the bed. "I'm not too young." He had been crying.

Angel's stomach tightened and she heard the erstwhile alarm speed up.

"Angel," the nurse started, "take deep breaths. Deep, calming breaths." Had she given this woman permission to call her Angel? Wasn't that what one needed before doing that? Why wasn't she Mrs. O'Shea anymore?

"Mom." Jason, her firstborn, stood at the foot of the bed, touched her feet through the thermal blanket. "What do you remember?"

She didn't want to remember, would evade the

question again. "Where am I?"

He shot a look at the nurse, then his brothers. "Parkland. Dallas."

Parkland. The teaching hospital. Where they sent the worst of the worst. "Oh, shit." She didn't curse in front of the boys. Not usually, even though they were grown and she'd just heard--and not chastised him for it--William be as foul as his father and grandfather ever had been.

She studied the blanket over her abdomen. How had she gotten here? And why?

"What day is it?" She lifted her eyes to Travis.

"It's Monday, Mom."

Monday. What happened to Saturday and Sunday? Dare she ask?

"What do you remember, Mom?"

This must be a really important point because so far everyone had wanted to know what she remembered. The nurse shot her a skeptical look, not expecting her to remember anything. Well, *Angel* could remember. If she tried.

She sighed, closed her eyes and rested her head on the pillow.

"Mom?" It was William, panic in his voice. He still knelt on the floor.

"Get up, William."

He stumbled to his feet and now she felt his hand on her head, which felt more and more like it was in a vise. "It'll be okay, Mom," he said.

Oh, God, that did it, her baby comforting her. It was bad. Something was very, very bad, but she didn't have the nerve to ask, to know for sure. She concentrated.

"I remember the dance Friday night. And your

Daddy's new car. Paulina got the keys early in the night." She was so tired. Did she have to open her eyes again? If she didn't, if she waited long enough, could she wake up in her own bed and it be Saturday morning? Because, she didn't really want it to be Monday. "And Daddy was upset because it was his birthday and he wanted a party. But, we're giving him one." Now she opened her eyes. Her three sons were watching her like an old cat at a mouse hole. Any sign of movement and they'd jump all over it. "Aren't we?" She creased her brow and her head hurt even worse. "Didn't we?"

The three of them passed around a horrified look.

"It's Monday," she repeated, then struggled to concentrate on remembering like they all wanted her to do. "Friday night, well, Saturday morning, early, we left the club. Daddy hadn't wanted to clean up, but Angel O'Shea always leaves her parties clean. Always." Two days were gone from her life. Had she been here for two days? Where were... "And Paulina was driving and Daddy was telling her about the engine, some ratio or other, and Eric and I were in the backseat, threatening to go to sleep if they didn't find a livelier topic, and..."

It was coming back to her. The dark highway, the second curve after the club cut-off, the bridge in sight, Mark's voice a drone. The deer. A doe, Paulina hitting the brakes, Eric's warning that where there was one there were two. The buck, the beautiful buck bounding across the highway after the doe, then just as Paulina sped back up, laughing at the near-miss, another doe, and this one she hadn't been able to avoid.

Paulina had yelled, frightened, even as she fought for control of the car. Mark had grabbed at the wheel, then thrown his arms up over his face. Eric had grabbed her and pulled her toward the center, but her seatbelt had pulled her back, as the car flew through the air, down the embankment. Trees and brush and the sound of the river.

And then she was here, eighty miles from where she last remembered.

She'd start with a simpler question then. "Where's Paulina?" She didn't mean to whisper, but the words wouldn't make themselves louder.

William and Travis pivoted their heads to their older brother. "She didn't survive the accident, Mom."

He wasn't volunteering anything, now was he?

"And Eric?" She barely had breath and that damn monitor was skyrocketing.

"He's here, Angel."

Her eyes roved to the new voice, fixed on Eric. He was in a wheelchair, Ty behind him, his hands gripping the handles. Eric's right arm was in a sling and there were bandages on his face. His right eye was black and his nose looked broken. Ty rolled him closer to the bed.

"Do I look worse than you?" she whispered.

He nodded. "Considerably. I'm so good they're letting me out." His voice was raspy.

She wet her lips, concentrated on Eric now, rather than her children. If she had to know the worst about Mark, she didn't want them to have to tell her.

"Where's Mark, Eric?"

Oh, God, let her wake up in her own bed with Mark all over her and the alarm ringing. Please, please, please! Please let Eric tell her he was in the next room.

"He's dead, Angel. Just like Paulina."

And the alarm went wild.

***

Eric clasped Angel's hand in his own, brought it to his forehead and cried with her. Granted, his injuries weren't as serious as hers, but in another way, he was much worse off. He hadn't had the solace of being unconscious at the scene of the accident, of not knowing until now.

He had awakened to a flashlight being shone in the window and a scramble of voices. He couldn't seem to work his right hand to unlatch the seatbelt and his left was trapped under him. The deflated side air bag was further hindering him. There was tapping on the window, asking if he could open the door, even as the emergency personnel were coming in the front. Then someone had him around the shoulders and all he could still do was strain towards Paulina, call for her, but she didn't answer. Her head was... not right on her shoulders. Mark, he couldn't see, and Angel looked like a rag doll.

They put him on a gurney. He didn't want to lie down, he *couldn't* lie down. He had to get to Paulina. Didn't they understand? He couldn't breathe, then he was breathing too hard and they put a mask on him, kept telling him to calm down. It just wasn't going to happen. He fought them, fought to get to Paulina, heard someone call his name, felt fingers on his face, felt someone turn his face to theirs.

"Mr. Eubanks."

How did they know who he was?

"Mr. Eubanks." It was a man in a uniform but he couldn't tell what type. "We're taking care of your wife, sir. You be still. Please. Don't injure yourself further."

He hadn't injured himself in the first place. There was... there was a... something in the road that did it.

Paulina was driving. Paulina was driving too fast.

He finally gave up on the effort and did as asked, let their words drift over him as he slid into and out of consciousness. Words he didn't want to remember, words he didn't want to understand. Broken neck. Severe trauma. Internal injuries. Two dead.

Then he was being loaded into a helicopter without knowing how he had been carried to it. The wind. The noise. Angel was already aboard. There were bags of liquid and tubes attached to her. Her face was swollen. Where was Paulina? Mark?

As he came to in the hospital Saturday morning, he saw his sisters. Since Ellen lived in Oklahoma City and Evie in Houston, he shut his eyes to the probability that this was a social call. His mother and Ty weren't with them, raising the ante higher that this was very bad news indeed.

Ellen, his older sister, took his left hand in hers, his right being incapacitated in a splint. He hadn't yet made sense of whether or not it was broken. It just hurt like the devil and was definitely going to put a crimp in his business for the summer. It looked like Paulina would have her boss-as-supervisor wish after all.

Evie, his younger sister, stood at the foot of the bed and sniffled. She was forty, way too old for sniffles. So, had the real tears been cried out? Both sisters looked to have aged since he saw them at Easter. Ellen's hair was a gray mess--between husbands she was usually more careful with her appearance--and Evie had hers back in a most unbecoming style, even for a harried mother with three stair-step children under the age of ten. She and her spouse had probably drawn lots to see who came to give him the bad news. It appeared Evie had won and got to leave the family nest. God, if he could be mentally chastising his siblings for their appearance then he was truly in avoidance mode.

"Eric." Now Ellen sniffed.

What could they talk about that wouldn't have him knowing for sure what he knew already? Should he ask about the weather because he didn't want to know why they were really here.

"Sis." He closed his eyes.

"Eric, sweetheart, look at me."

Sweetheart. Hell, she was in mother-mode. For a childless career-woman, it was a stretch. But he opened his eyes.

"Honey," she swallowed, "you were in an accident."

No shit, Sherlock. But he didn't say that, just nodded, although it hurt like hell, all the way from his head to his groin.

"Paulina," she wet her lips, shot a look at Evie. Paulina wasn't the one they would have picked for his wife, for their sister by marriage. It had always been an antagonistic, evil stepsister relationship, mutual between the three of them. If Paulina were dead... Ellen and Evie wouldn't be happy, would they? "Paulina didn't make it, sweetie. She didn't survive the accident."

Ellen's palm was sweaty, or was that his? She clutched at his hand now with both of hers. "I'm so sorry, Eric."

"So sorry," Evie repeated.

Paulina dead? Paulina wouldn't die. It wasn't in her game plan. But he knew, even as he didn't want to hear it. No. That would mean... that would mean Ty didn't have a mother. He didn't have a wife.

"No." He looked from sister to sister.

Evie set up a constant bobble with her head.

"Yes, honey." Ellen patted his hand now. "Your minister is outside. But we wanted to tell you, to be with you. We'll get him." Evie started toward the door.

"No." He called her back. *Minister?* "Evie, we don't have a minister."

She turned, brushed her hands down her jean-clad thighs. "So, okay, it's the O'Shea minister." She took deep breaths. "This is when you realize you should have been going to church," she said in a rush.

"Evie!" Ellen exploded. "Now is not the time!"

Evie pressed her lips together as if to hold in the words. One more bone of contention between his sisters and his wife: Paulina thought organized religion a sham and he'd taken the path of least resistance, gone along with her. They had allowed Ty to make up his own mind, to go to church with William, so Ty had taken the church social route. Therefore, the minister was really Ty's.

But he had no patience for this. "What about Ty?"

"He knows," Ellen said, gratefulness for the change in subject evident in her voice. "The O'Shea sons were all over that situation."

Mark and Angel. Oh, good Lord, were they dead too? "Mark? Angel?"

"Mark didn't make it." Could Ellen not say the word 'dead'? "Angel's in intensive care. They don't know. She's not awake yet."

"Can I get the preacher?" Evie said through clenched teeth.

"Yes," he sighed. There would be no peace until she did.

Evie almost ran this time.

"Mom?" he asked.

44

"She's with Ty until Paulina's folks get here. They were on a cruise."

God, yes. Now he remembered. Bargain basement cruise between Galveston, Cozumel and Key West. His father-in-law would most likely want him to reimburse the part of the trip they'd lose.

At least he didn't have to be present for their homecoming. "So, what day is it?"

"It's Saturday, babe. Noon."

Twelve hours earlier he had had a wife, friends as close--closer--than kin. Twelve hours before he had accused his wife of not loving him. And now he couldn't make it up to her, couldn't take it back. "I need Ty."

"We'll get him. We just thought… he's wanted to come."

"Now, Ellen. I need him now."

"Okay, babe. I'll call Mom. She'll bring him down."

He turned to see Reverend Johns walk purposefully through the door. At last, someone who could take charge. He pulled a stool to the side of the bed and from there Eric really didn't remember the rest of the day.

They expected him to make plans, to have an opinion on Paulina's funeral. How could he bury his wife when he couldn't leave the hospital? Monday, they told him. Release on Monday. And so it was. But he had to see Angel first and they said she was coming out of the coma. He could talk to her but there was no other comfort he could offer but the sympathy which came with having known for three days what she was just finding out.

Now he held Angel's hand and relived the pain in her tears. Where was the justice in this? Two families torn into pieces. He couldn't think; he couldn't plan. How was he supposed to be the leader in this? Travis and Jason had already looked to him about Mark's funeral. Bless their hearts, as Evie had continually said, they didn't know what to do.

Why did anyone think he did?

The boys had an uncle, Mark's younger brother, Marshall. He had arrived on Sunday from California, offering the boys guidance and a strong male family member. Mark's dad, Marcus, was in "poor health," the O'Shea family euphemism for a drinking problem, and his second wife--or was it his third?--had had the good sense to stay home. Mark's mother had done nothing but cry. So, the O'Shea sons, two of them grown but out of their depth and level of experience, looked to him, because they knew him better than they did their uncle. They were torn between worry for their mother and concern for their grandparents and he was familiar, an anchor in their rocked world. Although Angel's parents lived thirty miles away, they had taken over the house, made the boys feel uncomfortable in their own home. Eric knew they had decamped to his house, where an armed camp already existed between Paulina's parents and his mother.

And he yearned to go home?

Yes, with all his being. He wanted to shut them all out. He wanted to lock the door to his and Paulina's bedroom and gather their pillows together and ease himself onto their bed. He wanted to wallow in self-pity and indecision.

And then he wanted to wake up and find it was all a nightmare.

Instead, he would kiss Angel's hand and dry her tears. He would give his place over to her parents who were standing at the foot of the bed, their eyes full of their daughter, their *living*, awake daughter. He would let Ellen drive him home, and he would clean up as best he could with Ty's help. Then he would go to the funeral home, and he would make himself do what heretofore had been unthinkable.

Chapter 6

Tuesday morning

Angel would not be allowed out of the hospital for Mark's funeral.

Quite simply, the answer was 'no.' *No* from the doctors. *No* from her parents. *No* from her sons. Theirs at least was a reluctant no. They wanted her there, she could tell, but the evidence was mounting that she couldn't go. She wasn't strong enough. It was too far away. She had too many injuries.

"What if something pops, Mom?" William had asked, fear making his blue eyes wide and dark. "What if you..."

What if she died, too?

So, she wasn't going. The goose-egg size lump on the left side of her head was a major concern. She wasn't hearing well out of her left ear and her rotator cuff was torn. They'd not even let her up for the bathroom yet, but she was going to take care of that when the shift changed. Therefore, tomorrow her sons and their grandparents would bury her husband of twenty-five years and she wouldn't be there. They had been making the plans Sunday, coming to the realization that even if she woke up, she wouldn't be well enough to be there.

Mark is... Mark *was*. Oh, God. She turned her face to the pillow and started to soak it with tears again. She'd dismissed them all, made them leave. Her sisters, the caretakers *du jour*, had worn out their welcome five minutes inside the door. Didn't she want to know...? She didn't want to know anything else. She didn't need to be told anything else. She knew enough, thankyouverymuch. What--*who*--she wanted she couldn't have.

Not even one last look.

So how was she to remember Mark? Scowling Friday night on the steps of the club? Telling Paulina how to handle the Jag *just so*? Laughing when William was born? Crying when they'd found out she was pregnant with Jason? Angry when she was pregnant again so soon after and he had to adjust his college dreams yet again?

How did one remember half of one's life, half of one's self?

Her sobs broke again just as the door creaked open. Thank goodness there were no guns in the hospital; she would shoot the first female relative to cross the threshold.

"Angel, are you awake?"

A male voice, belonging to someone who had surely heard her cries, and was still enough of a gentleman to ask if she were awake.

Eric.

She sniffed and rubbed her eyes on the top edge of the sheet. "Yes, Eric."

He wheeled himself in.

"You're not walking?"

"Something's twisted in my hips. I can walk, but it

hurts. I came in for a scan. They'll hunt me down with the news."

"Where are your keepers?"

He smiled. "With yours in the cafeteria. Biting nails." He stopped beside her bed, reached through the rails for her right hand with his left, covered it. "Feeling any better?"

She shook her head. "Not physically. Not mentally…" Her voice trailed off. "Will I ever feel better?"

His blue eyes searched hers. "They say you do."

"That's what they say." She closed her eyes, slowly opened them. Eric was slightly out of focus. "Is William still at your house?" She blinked and he was clear.

"It's no problem. He can stay as long as he needs to, which will probably be until you get home. Ty likes having him there. I think it gives each of them protection from their relatives." He fiddled nervously with her fingers. "Evie dropped the two of them off at Travis and Jason's apartment before bringing me here. They'll bring him over when they get home from work."

"I told them to go back to work. To school. Not to worry about me. Jason can't miss class. They need normal."

"They'll be okay, Angel. Staying with all the grandparents…"

"Even I don't want to do that," she whispered. "But I've been lying here worrying."

"Don't worry about the boys."

"Not about them. Oh, of course about them. But the stores too." She concentrated on the two vases of pink roses on the wide window ledge. Wasn't there just one yesterday? How rapidly were they multiplying? The house must look like a funeral home. Didn't people have better things to do with their money?

"What about the stores, Angel?" Eric's voice brought her back to the subject she'd begun. "Yancey has it all under control, I'm sure."

She turned her head to look at him. "Or he will until Marcus Senior goes down and tries to remember how to run it. Or Marshall, who shook the sand from his feet so fast Mark thought it was a dust storm, decides to go in and take over. It's payroll week. I need to see Yancey."

"You need to not worry. They'll close tomorrow for the service. We can tell Jason to talk to him, tell him to come see you."

"Yes, that would do. I'm glad they're working. Mark would want it to stay open." She smiled weakly. "He'd even begrudge them the funeral time."

"My crews are working. Not tomorrow. But yesterday, today." He shifted in the chair, drew a deep breath. "I came to ask a favor."

"Anything, Eric. Anything you want."

"Listen to it first, Angel." He studied the blanket across her body. "They're not letting you out of here for the funeral." It was a statement.

"I know. It's just as well." She knew it was. Didn't like it, but facts were facts. "William is terrified something is going to happen to me now."

He nodded. "Angel…"

"Just say it, Eric. We have too many years between us for whatever you have in mind to upset me." She sighed. "And certainly not now. I don't have that much energy."

He nodded, interlaced their fingers and looked at her. "I think it's too much to have two funerals, one in the morning, one in the afternoon. Even a day apart. It's too much on our families who'll go to both. Too much on our friends since they're all the same. Do you... do you mind if there's just one service? Reverend Johns has agreed to it. Would Paulina be horning in?"

She sputtered a laugh. Was this what gave rise to his anxiety? "She'll rise from the grave if you roll her casket in front of the altar of a church."

"I have thought of that. But funerals aren't for the... for the dead. They're for the living. I figure I can explain it to her hypocritical ass later. Anyway, it's an urn. She wanted to be cremated." He pulled his hand from hers and shaped an object less than a foot high. "It's just a little pot. Won't take up much room." And now the bedeviling grin came. "I got it wholesale."

She laughed until the tears came and her head hurt even worse. "But I can't be there, Eric. I can't be there to see..."

He started laughing too.

"It's not fair. I can't be there!" She clutched her stomach. "This is absurd. I have to quit. It hurts. I swear, the laughter hurts."

He sobered his features. "Thank you, Angel."

"No, thank you, Eric." She bit at her lip. "I didn't think I'd ever find Mark and Paulina funny again."

***

There had been much laughter. After their first tenuous "double date" as Angel had styled it, after Paulina had gotten over the fact that she could indeed have fun with people she'd never thought to know, after William and Ty had been born a week apart, then there had been much laughter.

Angel settled into the hospital bed and eyed the morphine drip. She could dose herself, but since last night she hadn't. She needed a clear mind if she were going to make it out of here as soon as possible, a clearer mind if she were going to combat the force that was her family. So instead of dosing herself and sliding into oblivion, she would think about the laughter.

Cancun, seven summers ago. Jason and Travis were old enough to be left by themselves at the house, although she had her misgivings. She tacked a list of chores on the bulletin board, threatened to have their grandmothers stop by every day, and so obtained promises of good behavior. Ignorance would be bliss, Mark assured her. They left William with her mother and Ty was sent to Eric's. It was a four-day, three-night adventure at an all-inclusive German-owned resort, and the longest she had been away from her children since William was born.

The plane was crowded. Paulina hit the Mexican customs button, and it turned red instead of the go-ahead 'we know you're honest' green. All of their luggage had been subject to search. Their resort was the last stop on the tour company's hour-long route, and it would be the first pick up on Sunday morning. But two margaritas and a large serving of guacamole later and she had forgiven it all.

They left the resort once for dinner. Other than that, they went to the night club each evening, enjoying the music and atmosphere, even if Mark had to be pulled to dance and Eric didn't know when to quit. They slept past noon and stumbled to find the coffee. The pool was family-friendly, but the beach was private with a shallow sand bar which afforded the ability to walk out quite far. The resort's clientele was predominantly European, on holiday on the Mexican Riviera. Topless was the order of the day and the four of them--appropriately poolside attired--sat under a palm tree and tried very hard not to gawk at what was showing, all the while liberally commenting.

"She shouldn't."

"He shouldn't."

"What are they thinking?"

"Interesting tattoo." They followed the tilt of Paulina's soda can. Eric and Mark each slugged a big gulp of beer. Said tattoo started between the curvaceous young woman's shoulder blades and wound its way down her back bone, disappearing into her very brief bikini bottoms.

"I wonder if it emerges on the other side." Mark exaggerated his breathing.

"I think you need a dip in the water to cool you down," Angel told him.

"Let's go back to the room and you can cool me down."

"Don't let us stop you," Eric smirked, then dove for Paulina, grabbing her around the waist and pulling her to him. She kicked and sand flew over the towels. Angel's margarita spilled and they all ended up in a heap, laughing and spitting sand.

"Oh, I am sooo nasty sticky!" Paulina broke loose from Eric and stood, brushing sand from her slim thighs. There used to be many things Angel envied about her friend, but she'd matured beyond most of them. She doubted she'd ever mature beyond the envy of Paulina's ability to eat like a bear approaching hibernation and still look like a bird. "I'm going to rinse off!" Paulina headed to the waves as Angel stood and shook out her pareo, making sure the sand landed on Eric's feet. "And since it interests you all so much, I'm going to go topless!" Paulina called back to them.

"Did she just say what I thought she said?" Eric stopped in mid-brush.

"Not Pauli." Mark started shaking out the towels, brushing himself off. "Pauli goes topless, dinner is on me when we get back."

"I choose the restaurant."

"Sure."

"It'll be expensive."

"But she'll have to wear a top."

Angel rolled her eyes. There was always a bet going on. She turned to watch Paulina march into the surf. She bent over and washed the sand from her legs, then walked further out. Her two piece suit was red, a tankini befitting a woman in her late thirties, conservative but eye-appealing.

Just as the water covered her breasts, she turned to them and skinned the tank top over her head. She shrieked as a wave hit her back--and the tank flew out of her hand. It took a few seconds for Angel, Mark, and Eric to register what had just happened and then they laughed so hard they fell on top of each other. Paulina, in the meantime, had crossed her hands over her breasts and was yelling at Angel to help her.

"I don't know," Eric wheezed, "maybe we ought to see how Ms. Tough Talk gets herself out of this problem."

"She'll kill you. Anyway, it's me she's yelling for."

"Are you sure?" Mark cupped his ear. "I think she's

saying come on in, the water's fine."

"You two are going to be in such trouble." Angel untied her pareo and handed it to Eric. "Go be a man and rescue your wife. I'd be drowned before I can get to her."

"We're not going to hold this against her or anything, are we?" he asked as he started off.

"Nah, we'll let her forget."

But of course they never had. And each summer after for their annual retreat to Cancun, Paulina packed a one-piece.

This year, they were to have left next Thursday.

Chapter 7

Wednesday

It seemed everyone had an opinion on the music for the funeral. Eric himself was ill-acquainted with modern Christian music, knew Paulina would hate it, and hadn't a clue as to Mark or Angel's views. But he was tired of his mother's raised eyebrows, of his mother-in-law's sulk, of the resentment evident in every breath taken by Mark's mother. So he turned the entire thing over to the boys and the choir director.

From the beginning, Ty had begged to go with William to church camps. William was, from Ty's point of view, having loads of fun, while he was being punished with swimming lessons and weeks with his grandparents. For all her maligning of conventional churches, Paulina had not the heart to tell him no. She was going to raise a child who could make up his own mind, and now with thirteen-year-old Ty, the fruit of that conviction was showing. But on the religion question, it wasn't that she didn't believe, she just didn't believe in practicing as everyone else did.

So it wasn't a total farce to see her urn beside Mark's casket. Eric had no doubt God would understand and had already dealt with Paulina accordingly. And when it was Eric's turn, he would hear about it too.

Perhaps a better place for the funerals would have been the high school gym. The church was one of the larger in town, but today, it was standing room only. Eric insisted on walking in the side door from the minister's office where both families had squeezed in for prayer. His right arm in a sling, he was clumsy with the crutch, but Ty was on one side of him and William on the other.

He had picked up another son. The boy wouldn't sit with his brothers who escorted their grandmothers and sat on the other side of the center aisle. It didn't matter, Eric thought, as they scrambled to help him sit on the church cushion, taking his crutch and laying it down on the floor. He patted each one on the knee and felt them tremble. He glanced around Ty to Paulina's mother and saw the familiar set of the jaw, the stare into space that belied the ticking of the wheels behind it. Betty Powers was working up to a showdown with someone, and Eric doubted it was God. He would have scrunched down in the pew but it hurt too much to move.

The service was starting. The organ music dissolved and a lone voice reached out to the congregation. The words muddled together for him, but one of the boys sobbed and then the other and he found himself doing his best to hold two young men.

He knew what it was to lose a dad, Emil Eubanks succumbing to cancer when Eric was ten. Had he cried like this? It was a blur, a week's worth of memories he'd packed up and forgotten where he'd stored.

He felt a hand on his shoulder, a thumb trace up the back of his neck. His mother, sitting behind him, lending him what strength and comfort she could. He acknowledged her by tipping his head back and into her palm.

Oh, God, he prayed, *give me an hour's strength. Just an hour. Just enough to hold these two boys together. But you have to know, at the end of that, I'll be back asking for one more.* That seemed to be the only way he would get through this, an hour at a time. Maybe when Angel came home, it would be better. William would go to his mother and eventually, everyone would go home.

He lifted his head to concentrate on the minister's words. After their initial outbursts, William and Ty straightened up and eased from his touch. Yes, it would get better.

How could it get any worse?

Wednesday evening

Eric opened his refrigerator, surveyed his choices for dinner from the mounds of food brought by neighbors and friends. He thought he was hungry; there was a familiar gnawing in the pit of his stomach. But nothing tempted him to touch it. Nothing until his eyes lit on a brightly colored dish. Lifting the lid he found enchiladas. Miguel's wife. Bless her, bless her. She knew his weakness, and she had responded to it.

"What are you doing?" Melba Eubanks stood in the kitchen doorway.

"I'm hungry, Mom. Stella makes the most wonderful--"

She nodded and walked briskly to him, taking the dish and ordering him with a flick of her hand to limp over and be seated at the breakfast table. "I meant you want something, Eric, just ask. You don't need to be waiting on yourself. I'm still here. You know your sisters would have stayed if they could, but Ellen needed to get back to work and Steve was calling Evie every three hours with some complaint or other. He should have thought about handling those children by himself before he went to merrily getting her pregnant."

There wasn't much of an answer to that. "I'm just grateful they could come at all." Ruffles jumped into the dining chair beside him and looked over the table's edge.

"I can't believe Paulina allowed that cat's behavior."

"She didn't. Ty did." He tipped the chair and Ruffles flounced out with a sharp meow.

That seemed to satisfy her and she continued with the first conversation. "It's what family's for, hon. I'm here now. I'll take care of you."

For how long? he wanted to ask. He grimaced as he eased back into the kitchen chair. He watched her busy herself with a plate, put a generous portion of food on it, cover it, and put it in the microwave. His efficient mother, capable of raising three children on her own while holding two secretarial jobs and carefully investing the insurance money left by her husband, had not intended to work all her life. For her children, it was get an academic scholarship to college or get a job, a strategy which paid off. She had retired completely last year and taken up golf and travel with other widows. But Eric had known for months that she was getting bored. Might she find his present circumstance the answer to a higher mother-calling? He didn't think he could stand it, all the fussing about, the straightening up, the predictable meals on a schedule. He wanted his life back, the casual, this-is-your-first-warning way Paulina handled a crisis, the meals that he was just as likely to bring home from the grocery as was she.

What would it be like to be in this house alone, just

he and Ty? If it were too lonely, maybe they could borrow William sometimes. No, they couldn't do that. Angel would need him.

It wasn't that he had wanted only one child. He hadn't. He would have settled for four or five--obviously he had *settled* for one--but Paulina had definite ideas about the size of their family. One. One to bear, one to birth, one to educate. She had been an only child, and it hadn't hurt her. He wisely held his tongue--but quirked his eyebrow--the first time that point was made, and she never made it again.

But he thought he had her that first Cancun. She was playful, spirited, the way she'd been in college when they'd had more dreams than sense. He was going to be an artist working in multi-media but specializing in oils. In fact, his early work garnered praise and gallery showings even before they graduated. She had always had the law in mind. She'd specialize too, entertainment law, intellectual property. What a couple they would make!

But sense trumped dreams at every turn. Art doesn't always pay the rent in the best of times. They knew it was a fickle field, so to pay the bills, he worked for a landscaper when she entered law school. He found he was very good, that his artistic sense could work in the media of grass and flowers just as easily as oil and canvas. In the off-season, he took a horticulture class at the junior college and brushed up on his high school Spanish so he could better communicate with the laborers. Paulina thought it a passing obsession, but as she graduated with her JD, he was given the opportunity to buy the business from a man whose last heart attack put him on the retirement fast track.

To his wife's consternation, Eric took out a loan from the bank and one from his mother, and Eubanks Landscaping, with its self-acknowledged groaner of a motto, "U can bank on us", was born. He knew Paulina was disappointed in him, felt he had given up on his artistic potential. The household begun on one dream slowly evolved into two separate lives, as she forsook the practice of law altogether in her quest for independence and a better living in financial services, aka, a stock broker. She brought the energy to it that she brought to anything she desired, and Paulina Eubanks quickly was running her own office.

But that first Cancun, the one when Paulina bounced happily into the surf and tore off her top, that long weekend she had shown a glimmer of what they'd lost. Back in their room, he teased and cajoled her, plied her with kisses and a massage... and asked about another baby. Her eyes had widened and he thought she was going to acquiesce ("We can call her CC for Cancun," he'd whispered, "Nobody will know but us."), but she shook her head.

"I'm almost forty."

"We'll go to a specialist."

"What if I have twins? Older women have twins."

"We'll hire a nanny."

"Older women also have more Down Syndrome babies."

There was no argument for that and in the end, they'd just taken a nap.

Now he nodded as his mother put the plate of steaming food in front of him, knife and fork positioned just so. "Want a beer, honey?"

"Sure, if there are any." A house with so many

strangers and relatives in it for four days... his Friday night beer supply would have been woefully inadequate.

"A couple of cases showed up yesterday afternoon, courtesy of someone named Micky J."

His second crew's foreman, Miguel being chief of the first one. Between the enchiladas and what he was sure was his favorite brand of beer, the guys deserved a raise.

The enchiladas were primo, even reheated. The beer was ice cold. And still his stomach felt like it housed a boulder. He had to get some things out of the way with these people in his house. He would start with the easiest target, the one most likely to forgive him, and she was conveniently pulling out a chair and sitting at the table with him.

"Honey."

Dare he hope she would beat him to the punch?

"We need to discuss some things."

Maybe she was clairvoyant. Mothers were supposed to be, weren't they? Know when their children needed them? There wasn't an age limit to that, was there?

"I know we do."

She covered his left hand with hers. "I don't think you know it all." She scooted her chair closer and leaned to whisper. "Betty has been going through Paulina's things." She drew back and looked at him down the length of her nose.

"What?"

"Betty," she leaned closer again as she said his mother-in-law's name, "has been rifling through the jewelry." She popped back and straightened in the chair. "There. I've said it!" She pressed her lips together.

There was more?

"And that cousin of hers..."

"Cassidy?" he asked. There had been several distant relatives show up for the funeral, relatives so distant he had never met them. Surely they didn't smell a giveaway? Did they think he didn't exist?

"Cassidy. That's right." She kept her voice low, as if they might enter the kitchen any minute. Last he'd seen of them they were by the pool. "Cassidy was in her closet."

"When was this, Mom?" Might as well ask. She was not going to be satisfied until it was said.

"Yesterday afternoon while you were gone to the funeral home. This morning when you were down here."

"You were with me down here."

"I set your sisters to keep an eye on them."

The laughter started deep in the rock that was his stomach and bubbled up through his throat. "So, Mom, what did she get? A power suit?" He would have to dispose of all Paulina's clothes. Maybe the easy way was to put them in bags and haul them to Cassidy's car.

"No clothes. As if Cassidy could squeeze her plus-size butt into Paulina's clothes. But Evie said Betty pocketed some jewelry. Mementos, she called them when she knew she'd been caught."

God, his head hurt. He would not fight his mother-in-law for whatever she found in Paulina's jewelry box. The good stuff, the very expensive--and she had a modest amount of it--was in the box at the bank.

"It's Ty's, you know," his mother continued. "For his wife."

"Well, technically, Mom, it's mine. Our wills do not stipulate any exact bequests."

"Still…"

"I know. Betty should not have taken it without

asking. I'll talk to her." Like hell, he would. And now, with his mother so proud of her little spy ring, he was going to have the heart to ask her when she was leaving?

Probably not.

But the house had to clear. His mom, Betty and husband Brady, cousin Cassidy, and half a dozen others were still in semi-residence. He could look at this request cum showdown as a cure for this particular headache.

"In fact, let's go find them now." He pushed away from the table and adjusted the crutch under his left arm.

"Are you finished with your food?" Was his mother now looking for an excuse not to confront the rest? Except she didn't know what he really had in mind.

"Leave it. I'll reheat it." He waited for her at the kitchen door while she dropped napkins over his plate. "C'mon. I need you to protect my six."

She cocked a well-plucked brow. "My back, Mom. You gotta watch my back."

She'd never leave now.

Chapter 8

Friday

"**M**om?" William didn't bother to knock, just cracked Angel's bedroom door and called softly.

She cautiously shifted her weight in the lounger, turning from the window where she wasn't watching anything at all. Not really. Their backyard was not a hotspot of activity on an early summer afternoon. But it was a diversion for her eyes, a rest from the hospital walls. They'd let her come home late Thursday evening and she'd relished the clean colors of her landscaped yard ever since.

"What, sweetie?"

"Grandma said for me not to bother you, to tell him to go away, but she doesn't know Yancey. He's downstairs and he needs to see you."

Of course, her mother would consider anyone associated with the business as beneath her purview. How the hell did her mother think Angel got to live like she did, raise three sons without working except at the store two days a week, have a landscaped yard and manicured nails?

And a totaled Jaguar?

By marrying the plumber's son, that's how. Pity all these years had passed and her mother still didn't understand the dynamics which were at work.

"Of course, I need to see Yancey. But I don't think I can get down the stairs without a great deal of effort."

"Grandma told you to stay in the guest room."

Little twerp! He'd hidden from his grandmothers for six days--and now he dared quote one of them! Angel bit her tongue. It had taken twenty minutes to get up the stairs last evening but she was determined to sleep in her own bed. Would that she could have slept. "Yes, Grandma's told me a great many things." Enough that the hospital almost looked inviting again. "Ask Yancey to come up here. And bring me a legal pad--no, bring two from downstairs. And pens. Tell Grandma we need coffee and an assortment of cake slices from what I saw in the kitchen. That'll keep her occupied and give her an excuse to come up."

William nodded as if he understood her strategy for keeping her mother occupied. "Is it okay if I go back over to Ty's house with him? Most of his relatives are gone."

"Sure." A week ago he would have yelled he was going to Ty's, no permission needed, and been out the door before she could have answered. But while he was still in highly-protective-of-mom mode, he obviously couldn't resist the dig about the relatives.

"And we might not be right there," he continued. "You know, like in five minutes. It might be longer."

They lived five blocks apart with no major thoroughfares to cross. They each had top of the line bicycles. "And that would be because--"

"Because Gilly McCabe moved in about halfway

between us."

"Oh." Miss McCabe, the latest junior high unattainable, was now within easy bike-by distance. Except, unless Angel missed her guess, neither of these boys would ever find her ilk unattainable. "Take Daddy's cell phone," she nodded toward the jumble on top of Mark's chest of drawers where he'd left his business phone charging last Friday, "in case you need anything. Then why don't you call Grandma when you do get to Ty's? That way she won't worry."

He ducked his head, scuffed at the carpet with the toe of his worn shoe. "Well, Grandma got me my own cell phone yesterday." He dug in his pocket and produced the slimmest model Angel had ever seen. "She said she wanted to know where I was all the time." He shrugged. "But she hasn't bugged me much. And we didn't know about using Dad's."

Angel tried to assimilate it. "This was Grandma's idea?"

"Sorta.'"

She closed her eyes and nodded. She didn't mind William having the phone; in fact, it had been a hot topic for family discussion, most of the controversy centering on just how smart a smartphone to allow him. "Write your number down." He scrambled to comply and handed her the slip of paper, kissing her forehead quickly.

"You're not upset with Grandma, are you?"

"No." But she feared her loss of control. "Don't forget Yancey and the paper."

He kissed her again and then skidded through the doorway, his weight clomping on the stairs.

She knew Ty and William had been inseparable this

week, bouncing back and forth between the houses, but mostly at the Eubanks'. William hadn't come with Travis and Jason to bring her home, but had, as her mother had succinctly put it, 'miraculously shown back up', within five minutes of her arrival. Because she had called him? The pity was that no one else had miraculously left within the same five.

Well, Marshall had already gone. He'd stayed for the funeral, did a screeching stop at the hospital to assure her that if she needed him, he'd return posthaste. He squeezed her hand, told her she was looking better, urged her to "hang in there, kid." At least he hadn't attempted to horn in on the stores.

She had managed to dismiss her sisters, too, but that was due more to old rivalries and years of alleged hurts and misdeeds than anything else. She believed the words she'd uttered from the top of the stairs after the ordeal to get her up there, were, "You two can go home now." And she hadn't added 'thank you for all you've done.' If indeed they had done anything but sit around and eat the donations of food, wonder if she'd miss a tube of lipstick or a bottle of nail polish if they 'borrowed.' There had been a great deal of stomping around and a slammed door, but even at Angel's insistence, they wouldn't have gone without their mother shooing them out the door. She'd have to give credit where credit was due. Alas.

She feared Yancey wanted to talk about yet another relative: Marcus Sr. The old man knew nothing of the current operations, but she'd bet he'd had his butt and his opinions behind the counter all week--and a beer just out of sight. He had the uncanny ability to show up when Mark needed him the least, the thirty or sixty mile drive from his current home to one store or the other being nothing if he were on the outs with the present wife, but an un-surmountable thirty or sixty miles if Mark had really needed his expertise. Besides that, someone had rifled through Mark's closet and there was only one candidate for that violation. Not even her sisters had that much nerve. She shuddered. He's the one that needed to leave, even before Mark's mother, who had taken over Jason's old room and allowed herself to be waited on as the grieving mother she was. Angel's dad had declared himself superfluous after this morning's breakfast and retreated back to his own place. Reluctantly, Angel had to admit she did actually need her own mother.

Or, to be more accurate, she needed someone. Stella and Miguel's college-age daughters would do better for helping her change her clothes and driving her to the doctor. Too, they could use the money for college expenses. She'd call Eric for their phone number as soon as she dispensed with Yancey.

There was a tentative knock on the door. Yancey stepped through. "Angel?"

She smiled at Mark's right-hand man, the manager of their first store, the man she was looking to to be the rudder for her unsteady boat.

"Come in, Yancey. Pull up a chair."

James Yancey was tall and raw-boned, a man with a bottomless stomach and a ready laugh to explain it: "I nervous it away." But he wasn't laughing today as he pulled the desk chair over a few feet from her and handed her the pads and pens. He put a lap top case on the bed as he sat, dwarfing the chair, and every piece of furniture in the room but the king-sized bed.

"I'm sorry to bother you, Angel."

"It's no bother. I have to find a new normal and

dealing with the store beats all the other normals I can think of."

He nodded. He was a few years older than Mark, a worthy successor-owner if it should come to that. "Don't worry none about the stores. They're doing fine. In fact, we've done more business. People coming in to offer condolences and see what they can do and not cause they need plumbing supplies." He looked past her shoulder to the sky visible through the window. Was he uncomfortable here in her bedroom? He would have to get over it. Or, was he uncomfortable because of what he'd come to say? "Angel, I don't want to burden you, but we've had some problems."

She lifted her hand, indicated for him to continue.

"Handy Plumber didn't want to deliver because they said they didn't know about the future of the stores and all. Whether they'd get paid."

She shook her head. "So much for building a reputation for paying on time and saving Handy Plumber's ass when they were about to go under. What did you tell them?"

"That you were the owner now and alive and well and gonna be mad as hell if they stiffed us."

She quirked a smile. "And?"

"We got our delivery." He indicated the laptop. "I downloaded the week's files to computer. I didn't know if you wanted to mess with them, but if you did..."

"Thanks, Yancey. I could have used them about three this morning when I couldn't sleep."

He gave her a nod of sympathy. "And the checkbook's in there too."

"It's payroll. I know."

He nodded again. "The guys came to me, as a group,

said to tell you not to worry. To wait until next week. Nobody was destitute--well, that damn kid Jakie can't keep a dollar in his pocket--but he lives at home."

"You have his check made out?"

He shrugged.

"You're too good, Yancey." She motioned for the checkbook and he opened the case and pulled it out, laid it on her lap. He clicked a ball point pen from his pocket and gave it to her, too, never mind the two pens he had handed her earlier.

Footsteps on the stairs and her mother appeared with three cups of coffee and an assortment of cakes on a wooden tray. "Yancey, you've met my mother, Delores Buttons?"

"Ma'am." He gave a quick nod of his head.

Delores balanced the tray on the ottoman which she pulled closer to them. She handed Yancey the first cup and looked wounded when Angel refused the second. She picked up the third cup. "I couldn't find any decaf, Angel."

"Should be some in the freezer."

"They must have drunk it all. I think I'll tidy in your bath." She took her coffee and disappeared through the door. Angel heard the towel cabinet opening and knew, despite the noise being made, that her mother was listening to every word.

For the moment, she concentrated on Jakie's check. And all the rest of them, dutifully filled out by Yancey and Teresa, the business office guru. "You have a heart of gold, Yancey," she told him as she flipped to the final page of checks.

"Not really." He gave the bathroom door a quick glance. Leaning toward her and lowering his voice, he asked, "When's the old man leaving?" He eyed the cake slices and selected one.

She grimaced. "How big a nuisance is he?"

"Handy Plumber? I beat him to that phone call by half a ring."

She noted the last running balance and returned the checkbook to him. "I'll take care of it."

He took a second piece. "I don't mean to cause problems in the family, but he's..."

"...Causing problems for the business." She finished the sentence for him.

"Do you want me as back-up?" He brushed his hands on a napkin.

"Do you want to be?"

He scowled. "Honestly? No, Angel, but I will. I don't think Jason is up to facing down his grandfather and no offense to your father, but..."

"It's okay, Yancey. I totally understand. And my dad's already deserted this ship."

The first battle of post-Mark. Of her new life. Of learning to be alone. Of not needing a man's back-up, no matter how well-intentioned.

"Well, there's one more thing." He studied his big hands, turning them over and picking at a callus on his thumb.

"Anything." She had a momentary picture of herself as potentate, Yancey a commoner come in supplication. And her mother the vizier on the other side of the curtain, listening to all and taking notes. She shook the image from her head. It must be the drugs... or lack thereof.

"The bank called about the loan application for Plumb, Land, and Sprinkler."

Angel still couldn't help but smile at the ridiculous

name for the joint venture Mark, Eric, Miguel, and Yancey cooked up over beers in the back of O'Shea's Plumbing Supplies one night in March. Eric had stopped by the main store, bemoaning the scarcity and price of plants grown and taken care of the way he wanted them to be. Mark had added his comments on the growing lawn sprinkler system business, and two six-packs later, Plumb, Land, and Sprinkler had been born. Mark and Eric would bankroll it on land Mark had bought for a third store. Miguel and Yancey would manage-to-own. The architectural drawings were done for a set of greenhouses, with a small store for gardening supplies but specializing in sprinkler systems. The utilities were cleared with the county and utility companies and the loan applied for.

"What did the bank want?"

"To know if we were going through with it." He put his coffee cup on the tray, didn't look at her.

She knew he asked as much for himself as for the bank. He was excited about this, and Mark's death must have brought his dreams of business-ownership to a screeching halt.

"I see no reason why not."

Something dropped—loudly—in the bathroom. Angel rolled her eyes at Yancey. He grinned ruefully.

"I just need to get in touch with the lawyer for the details. Ownership transfer. Probate. But call the bank and tell them we consider it business as usual on this end."

He took a deep breath. "What do you think about Eric?"

"I'll ask him, but I can't imagine he won't want this for himself and Miguel, too."

"Thanks, Angel." He stood, balancing the checkbook at his side. "Don't worry about the stores. We're taking good care of them."

"Trust me, Yancey. The stores have been the least of my worries."

He smiled. "I'll show myself out. Bye, Mrs. Buttons," he called in the direction of the bathroom door. "Thanks for the coffee and cake."

Angel heard his footsteps clear the bottom stair as her mother emerged from the bathroom. "You're not..."

Angel held a hand up to her. "Zip it, Mother. I am so not in the mood to argue. Life goes on. Business goes on."

Delores drew herself up and pinched her lips. "People will think you callous."

"People will think what they wish. We have two dozen employees and I will not hurt them nor their families."

Delores set her lips in a straight line and lifted the tray. "Do you want me to leave the cake?"

"No. Just find Marcus," no sense in attaching the Sr. any longer, "and tell him I need to see him, okay?"

She arched a brow. "Do you need me to call your father to come back?"

"No, Mother. I have to do this on my own." She paused. "And close the door."

***

The afternoon shadows lengthened across the backyard. Angel didn't move from the leather lounge chair. Household sounds filtered through the door and vents: the murmur of the TV in the den, the clanging of pots in the kitchen, slow footsteps in the hall which, thankfully, went away from her closed door. She shut her eyes. A week ago...

When would she stop thinking in terms of 'a week ago?' She'd spent the days in the hospital--when she was coherent, that is--recalculating time. A week ago, she'd begged out of closing the books at store #1 so she could meet with the florist. A week ago, she'd met with the club chef and tweaked the menu. A week ago, she'd stood in front of the mirror and shimmied into her blue dress as Mark had watched.

Where was that dress now? Covered in blood, stuffed in a hazardous waste bin, disposed of so it wouldn't contaminate? Her shoes, were they gone, too? What was she complaining about--she still had her feet.

Not that they were taking her many places. She needed to get up, to go to the bathroom. She needed to do the physical therapy exercises given her to rid herself of the stiffness. She needed to go back to bed. She needed to sleep.

Last night had been awful. Reaching out with her left hand, she could touch the hollow Mark's body left in the bed's down pillow top. They joked that no matter how hard they shook it or which way they turned it, their forms were still there. And they were. Even through the lightweight summer cover, she could see the indentations now. Should she move to the middle?

It wasn't that she had never slept without Mark. But she'd always been confident he'd be back from the golf trip, the Scout camp, the business meeting. Always. Then to lose him within a length of her own arm... To not even touch him in death...

Last night, she would have tossed and turned if such

movement had been easy. She'd allowed her mother to prop her on pillows and she'd laid on her back, staring at the darkened ceiling, marking the time by the off and on of the air conditioner. She thought about calling for Dweeb, for the companionship and warmth, but he was tucked up with William. She'd have had to get out of bed and go down the hall and that would have disturbed the rest of the house. She'd tried to read, but her mind couldn't absorb the words. She feared what she'd write if she worked on the thank you cards: "Dear Juliet: Thank you so much for the casserole. I wish it hadn't turned to sawdust in my mouth. But, no worry, the upside is I'll finally lose weight this way. Love, Angel"

No. It was definitely better she hadn't reached for the lists of food, of flowers, of memorials.

So she hunted down the remote control from its niche on Mark's side of the bed, but late-night TV was a bigger wasteland than she'd ever suspected. She couldn't summon the energy to get the laptop computer from her office desk in the next room, to let her fingers tap to her familiar internet news stops. Her mother had stacked last week's newspapers in a corner of the study "for later," but Angel feared what she would find on paper or web: Mark's and Paulina's obituaries, details of the crash.

Photos.

Her current bravura to her mother had been just that: a great show, a bluff. She had to hold things together. She had to hold herself together. No one would be served if she melted into the puddle she wanted to be. The doctors promised her the headaches would lessen, her soreness would go away. The ribs would mend. Her hearing in her left ear would clear. She'd eventually have full use of her arm. Food would taste good again. The bad dreams would disappear.

Another reason she hadn't slept. The dreams had come in the hospital, nightmares of the crash. Drug-induced, she had hoped, so she had stopped the medication as soon as possible. But it was still in her system. If she closed her eyes, she'd see the images, see Mark grab the steering wheel to avoid the third deer. She'd hear Paulina's terror-filled scream as the car plunged over the embankment. She'd feel Eric's hands and body as he tried to shield her, draw her into the middle of the backseat. She'd taste the blood in her mouth and then she wouldn't remember anything for over two days.

She couldn't sleep because her mind would dwell on what she could remember.

The knock on the door was not subtle when repeated. She realized she'd been hearing it, but paying it no mind because she was drawn into her own thoughts. "Angel, you okay?"

It was Marcus, gruff voice and rough exterior, the beta-version of the man her husband became. He didn't wait for her answer, but opened the door and leaned in.

"I'm fine, Marcus."

"Delores said you wanted to see me. Called me down at the store and told me to get back ASAP." He frowned, then tossed back the rest of the beer he held.

"That's right. Come in and have a seat."

She would survive because she had to.

Chapter 9

Eric rested his bare feet in the cool water on the steps leading into his backyard pool. He'd discarded the walking cast, even though looking at his battered right foot brought only a grimace. He had gotten himself down into this position, but he'd be damned if he could stand up and get himself out. He would have to wait until Ty came home from wherever he had disappeared to, most likely William's. Melba had declared them in dire need of milk and eggs and taken herself off to the grocery. Since she had been eyeing the weekend sales in the morning newspaper, he doubted she'd be right back. He'd left the house phone on the patio table which was two feet shy of the length of his crutch even if he laid on the tile and stretched. How pitiful was he?

His eyes skated over to the small wooden building at the back of the property, his 'studio,' or so Paulina had hoped it would be when it was built. In reality, it housed a beat-up desk, office phone and answering machine, and a draftsman's drawing table, where he did his designs. Occasionally, he would sketch, dig out an old photograph of Ty and try his hand once again. But he never showed them to Paulina. To do so would be to give her hope. False hope. He wouldn't do that, have her hope that he'd return to his roots, to oils and brushes and canvas, only to have that hope die. Now yard equipment the company no longer needed was pushed to the back, and the easels and boxes of artist's tools were pinned against the walls.

But as there was no sense following that line of thought, he tried mentally cataloguing what needed to be done with the landscaping. Even that was a useless endeavor, as he never had his own backyard tended to until there was no other work to be done. In the same vein as the cobbler's children not having shoes and the doctor's kids being perpetually sick, the landscaper's backyard was not the height of perfection. His front yard he kept in excellent condition as, he had listened to Paulina say often enough, it was his best advertisement.

Paulina.

Had it only been a week since the accident, since he'd insulted his wife? Since his life was normal?

He'd been back to the doctor again. X-rays, MRIs, EEGs, a CAT-scan. He wasn't given to vague complaints and being sick for no purpose. Hell, he couldn't remember the last time he'd been ill or laid-up. *Time, Mr. Eubanks,* they'd all told him. *You're just not used to being out of commission. Your system needs time. Time to mend. Time to recover.*

Time to forget.

Well, that last was his advice to himself.

Miguel had stopped by this afternoon. Eric watched his mother show his crew foreman in while she frowned at the pile of ledgers and files in his arms. He'd called Miguel and told him to come over. He was going nuts with nothing to do. They didn't work on Saturdays usually, but tomorrow he wanted to ride around and view the jobs. Ty was too young to drive and the idea of being trapped in the car with his mother... Well, there were worse fates, he supposed. There was his mother-in-law.

He smiled to himself.

Talk about something that hadn't been pretty. His arrival poolside Wednesday evening was greeted with deer-in-the-headlights looks from his "guests." Bad comparison. Deer scampering in front of the headlights is what had brought him to this sorry state of affairs in the first place. But he kept the comparison to himself .

The patio tables had been covered with liquor bottles and mixers. A bag of ice spilled into an ice chest and food was everywhere. He wasn't even sure which relatives the couple sunbathing together in the chaise belonged to, and the only attention they paid him was to adjust their sunglasses. He leaned on his crutch and sighed. He felt his mother behind him and, in an incongruous frame of mind, he mentally heard the blare of trumpets, the toreador's call to the bull.

He was a sick man because he enjoyed it.

"Everyone," he began. "Is this everyone in the house?" He scanned the faces he did know. "Brady, where's Betty?"

"Resting." His father-in-law opened the bottle of single-malt Scotch and poured himself another. Eric's stomach roiled. Prior to setting eyes on his son-in-law's liquor cabinet, Brady Powers' idea of a good Scotch was one someone else bought. A lifelong seeker of easy riches, Brady had left a string of get-rich-quick schemes in his wake as he stumbled toward retirement age. He was basically harmless because he was basically lazy. If not for Betty's talent with a ledger, which had ensured the family's financial footing from her long-time job with a mortgage company, the Powers family would have cratered. Brady had been delighted when his only child chose the law, ecstatic when she'd gone into financial services. Now, he told her, she could take care of them. Paulina's largesse had extended no further than Christmas and birthdays and their ever-rocky relationship became more so. No wonder Betty had been going through the jewelry.

Eric shifted his weight. His foot hurt. His arms hurt. His soul hurt. "Would you go get her? I need to speak to everyone and I'm tiring." Obviously, he was not above playing the crippled and scarred husband card.

Brady paused in his pour. "Well... she did just go."

"I'll get her, Dad." Ty was out of his chair and off in a flash.

Eric enjoyed everyone's discomfiture as he continued to stand, the sun bearing down, sweat beading on his forehead. Just as he was on the verge of giving in and sitting down under an umbrella, Ty appeared with his grandmother in tow.

"Yes, Eric?" She was breathless, as if she'd run a race. He couldn't believe she wasn't gone to her home 45 miles away already, gone to soak up the sympathy and tears from her friends who would commiserate with her on the loss of her only child. She couldn't be getting enough of that here.

"Have a seat, Betty."

She collapsed in a chair beside her husband.

Eric studied his audience one more time. "Ty and I appreciate everything you've done for us under these trying circumstances, but it's time for us to start putting ourselves back together. So, by the morning, I'd like to be able to say good-bye to each of you."

There was stunned silence. What did they think--that they could move in? Dare he add for Betty to empty her pockets at the entry hall tree, and would Brady please replace half of what he'd drunk--and not the cheap stuff either? That would be going too far. But what was the sense of living with an abrupt and bossy woman if some of it didn't eventually rub off?

If there wasn't going to be any comment--and really, what could they say?--he was getting out of the sun. He balanced himself on the crutch, and with Ty and Melba for escorts, he moved toward the French doors. Stopping for a second to retrieve his bottle of single-malt, he left them still open-mouthed.

To his great relief, by noon on Thursday, they were all gone except his mother. He was giving her until Sunday night, then he'd call in the big guns, Evie and Ellen. He knew his limits.

In the meantime, he was doomed to sit here with his feet in the water, listening to the phone's chirp and promising himself he'd never do this again.

***

"Dad, why aren't you answering the phone?" Ty propelled himself through the backyard gate, William in his wake, Dweeb in his. The boys bounced off their bikes, letting them drop to the ground, wheels spinning. Out of breath and red-faced, they ran to him, skidding to a stop at the water's edge. "Angel called William on his cell and said there was no answer here and for us to get over here now." He heaved several breaths and bent double, his hands on his knees. "Don't scare me like that,

Dad."

Oh, shit. "I didn't mean to."

"I mean, I was scared, Dad. You can't not answer the phone. You want to swim, you need to wait for me."

"I didn't..."

William retrieved a cell phone from his shorts pocket, hit a button and said 'mom,' shucked his shoes while he waited to be connected. Even in the midst of Ty's wrongful accusations, Eric was impressed. His phone didn't do that. "He's in the pool," William reported.

"No, I'm not." He held his hand out for the phone. Angel. He hadn't talked to her since Tuesday in the hospital. He realized with a twist in his gut that had nothing to do with the accident, that he *needed* to talk to her.

William handed the phone over and then followed Ty's example of shedding his tee shirt and completing a shallow dive into the pool. The boys splashed at the deeper end. Dweeb raced from one spot to the other, then plunged in with them. And he still sat with his feet in the water. Just call him Mr. Raisin.

"Eric?"

It was Angel's voice... but it wasn't. It wasn't the sure voice, the deliberate tone, the confident Angel he was used to. It was shallow, breathy. Confused.

"It's me."

"You're swimming?"

"No. I have my feet in the water and I can't get myself up and our two numskulls are acting like six-year-olds at the other end. They didn't give me a chance to explain." He paused. "I didn't mean to worry anyone. I just wanted to be outside."

She laughed, a weak-sister version of Angel's real

laugh, a throaty heart-felt spill that was usually followed by a lightweight punch to Mark's arm if he'd been the cause of it. "Outside really sounds good. I'm stuck in my room. And I've just had a terrible scene with Marcus."

He could very well guess what that was about. "Did you get your point across?"

"Yes. Oh, yes." He heard her shift her weight. "I think it's safe to say I've been cut out of the will."

"Do you," the idea came to him like an oasis in the desert, "do you want me to come over? As soon as the boys quit horsing around and help me get my feet out of the water and Mother gets back and can drive me, that is." He sounded like he was eight years old, one excuse after another, all of it hinging on a ride from mom.

Her laugh was fuller. "What a sorry lot we are. I'd rather come over there. You have more privacy, fewer accoutrements, or so I've been told."

"Are you able? Should you?" He felt protective, asking her questions he'd asked himself earlier. *Am I able to get in the water? Should I?* What he should have done was pursued it one more: *Can I get out?*

"Should I?" she echoed. "Who knows, but I'm coming. It will take an effort, but at least my mommy is at home."

That was the Angel he knew, quick and sarcastic, her wit not as biting as Paulina's, not as mean-spirited. She hadn't always gotten her way the first time out, but he'd be hard-pressed to find an example where Angel hadn't won a compromise.

He clicked the phone off. "Hey, numskulls!" He splashed at the water and got their attention. "Get me out of here." They swam over, all arms and elbows and powerful kicks. But helping him stand, they were overly solicitous, as if he would break.

"Where to, Dad?"

"The patio table. Crank up the umbrella," he instructed, as William eased him into the cushioned wicker chair. "Get some tea and glasses. See if there's anything in the kitchen to eat that's not gone offensive. Your grandmother's bringing your mom over, William, and we have to at least look like we can have guests."

"Gran will be home soon. She'll fix us up," Ty explained.

"You guys are quite capable of setting a table and finding food. And we have to start doing things on our own, Ty. It's the way of our world now." He looked at the boys, who were passing uncomfortable looks between themselves. "And well the two of you should know it."

***

They made quite a sight coming through the back gate, Angel's mother carrying her crutches, while William carried his mother.

"Honey, you shouldn't be doing this." Angel was protesting even as she clung to his neck with a death grip from her right arm. "You'll get a hernia."

"Better than growing old watching you crutch it through the gate and then fall when you get here." He settled her in the chair opposite Eric, propping her feet into another chair. He took the crutches from his grandmother, leaned them on the table edge. Drawing a deep breath, he made as if he could draw no more. "Please notice I didn't say a thing about how heavy you are which is what Travis and Jason would have done."

Before she could reply, he grabbed his grandmother's elbow and propelled her toward the French doors into the house. "Mrs. Eubanks just got back from the store." Ty held the doors open for them and they disappeared inside.

Angel tracked their progress. "I think I've just been insulted by my baby."

"Probably not the last time."

"Oh, I'll guarantee that." She turned her attention to him. "But since food has lost its flavor, in a just world, there'll soon be less of me."

"And is it a just world, Angel?" The question was out before he could stop it.

Her brows drew together and she pursed her lips. "I thought so until a week ago." She sighed. "Now, I'm not so sure."

His gut twisted. "Me, neither," he whispered.

"Which probably means I'll get fat as a toad."

"Angel," he scolded.

"Nah, it's okay, Eric. My humor's off a bit." She paused. "My everything is off a bit."

"Or a lot."

"Or a lot." She swept a hand down the house dress she wore, with its large pockets and snaps up the front. "I apologize for looking like something in a fifties commercial. It's about all I can get into comfortably."

"You look great. Just seeing you, Angel. You look great."

She wouldn't meet his gaze, seemed as embarrassed as he was by his raw honesty. She let her eyes bounce about the backyard. "You need a yard man."

A change of subject was always appropriate. "I'll ignore that." He didn't want to discuss the mundane; he needed the details. "Are you sleeping?"

"No." She shifted her weight in the chair and rubbed her right leg. "I'm doing nothing but thinking and not always coherently."

Better. He needed to hear this, to know he wasn't alone. He nodded.

"The boys." She nodded in the direction of the house. "How do you think they're doing? Really doing?" She turned troubled blue eyes to him, bit at her lower lip.

"Not worth a shit."

She nodded. "They're trying to act as if nothing has happened, but I think it's an act for me. Even Travis and Jason are nonchalant. I know that's not the case. I know they're torn up, but they won't let me in."

"Angel," he reached across the table toward her. "They'll come round. It's awful losing a parent. I know. But Jason and Travis are stepping up to the plate to protect you and William is following their example."

She acted as if he hadn't spoken. "And they can't come to you because you're hurting. And Marcus is such a bastard and my dad…" She sighed. "My dad doesn't say anything ever, so not talking about it is par for the course with him." She blinked and tears trickled down her cheeks. "What am I going to do?"

What was he going to do? It was the same question from the opposite side of the table. Ty was concerned, protective, and deep down scared witless, if his own experience was any count. Was losing a mother different from losing a dad? Had their sons lost different holds on their respective worlds? How would his life have been different if Melba had died and not his dad?

Angel was looking at him as if he had the answer to her question. "What are either of us to do, Angel? The boys will come round. Thanksgiving. Christmas. You'll serve the turkey and all of a sudden, it'll look like Niagara Falls."

"The hardest part is Mark's birth and death are nearly the same."

"Don't torture yourself."

She swiped at the tears and pressed her lips together. "Tell me about the funeral." She sniffed and straightened her backbone. An angel prepared for battle. "The boys don't want to talk about it, but I pressed Jason, and then Mark's mother wouldn't quit when she heard Jason telling me. She had to jump in there and correct him, but it was how he remembered it. I needed to know how he felt and it was the closest I got to any real feelings from him since I woke up at the hospital." She turned her attention to her tea glass and rubbed the condensation from the outside of it. "Now I need to know how you saw it."

How could he say it was awful without upsetting her?

"But only if you can tell me. If you can't…"

What would be one more male clamming up on her? But how could he find words which wouldn't have her grimacing, squeezing her eyes shut to block the tears she was now determined to hold back?

His silence brought more words from her. "I'm sorry, Eric. I've upset you and we can't do that to each other."

"No, Angel, you haven't. I'm just trying to decide where to start."

"Anywhere. The end, we'll go forward. The middle, we'll hop around. Just talk to me."

"Okay, then." He studied her, her anxious eyes, the worry lines on her forehead that Mark teased her about becoming permanent. "We'll start at the beginning." He wet his lips. He would begin the way the two couples had handled so many situations, with irony and a wink. "I knew Paulina was really dead when she didn't reassemble herself and go after Judge Hanson's throat when he came down to the rail."

Angel quirked a brow but kept a straight face. "You think he was making sure she was dead?"

"I imagine he was praying those were indeed her ashes."

It was working. She stifled a smile. "They didn't exactly like each other, did they?"

He shook his head. "He's part of the reason she quit the DA and went into financial services. The only man who ever made her run."

"But she did it with class and made a helluva lot of money. Spite has its rewards."

"So you'd think I could afford a yard man."

Clouds skittered in front of the sun and a breeze kicked up out of the north. It felt good on his skin, and Angel closed her eyes and tilted her head back. Could he get by with the snide Judge Hanson joke being his view of the funeral?

"Tell me, Eric."

Obviously he could not. She didn't look at him, but kept her eyes closed, rested her head against the wicker chair back. He'd thought this patio set an overindulgence when Paulina had insisted on it, but now it was as if a bit of his wife gave comfort to them both. Not that Paulina was in the business of making anyone comfortable.

"And you'll tell me about your conversation with Marcus?"

"Tit for tat?"

"You scratch mine…"

"Yes, I'll tell you about Marcus." She rolled her head to look at him. Her face was drawn, sallow. Her blue eyes lacked their usual brightness. Had he aged in a week the way she had? He'd been convinced Paulina would still be a looker at ninety while Angel was never going to age well physically. Today though, it was as if the next fifteen years had caught up with her in a week.

Should he gloss over it, paint a pretty funeral picture of kind words and organ music, stirring eulogies, a packed sanctuary? That was all true, but Angel didn't want, nor did she deserve, for him to skim the surface. She wanted the depths and only he could give them to her.

"It was awful. William sat with Ty and me. I tried to get him over with his grandmothers but he wouldn't go, and I wasn't going to make an issue of it. Betty looked like she could chew God up and spit him out. Someone in the back was sobbing, and I didn't think either of us had that many friends. Rev. Johns said all the right words and I guess we sang all the right songs. I couldn't stand. I couldn't sing for the knot in my throat. I sat there and sweated and prayed for the strength to come home. And then people just kept coming to shake my hand and say they were sorry and there could have been a thousand or just two and I swear, Angel, I wouldn't have known the difference. I was trapped and I wanted out."

Angel felt the tears roll down her cheeks. "I'm sorry, Eric. So sorry I wasn't there." So sorry she'd received the answer to her persistent question. What had she expected, a good fairy version of her husband's last rites? *Abracadabra--you go to Heaven?* And now she was supposed to condense one of the worst verbal exchanges of her life into a relevant equivalent?

She'd start the same way Eric had. But from there, where did she go? "Marcus and me. It was awful." She concentrated on the underside of the umbrella. It was a beautiful wicker set, six chairs, glass-topped table, a settee and ottoman. She'd wanted--no, desired, lusted after, coveted--one just like it, but Mark had been stubborn. She smiled to herself. What was she thinking? She could buy it now. Hell, she could even buy two and answer to no one about it.

But that smile disrupted the memory of her father-in-law.

"Delores said you wanted to see me. Called me down at the store and told me to get back ASAP." He frowned.

"That's right. Come in and have a seat."

"I'd rather stand."

"Suit yourself."

He tossed his empty beer bottle into her pretty shell wastebasket, then widened his stance and put his hands behind himself, military-style. She'd seen him do it for years, but still it disquieted her. His objective, no doubt. He knew why she wanted to see him. He was many things, but a fool was not one of them.

"Marcus," she had to choose her words carefully, "I know you've been helping at the stores this week." He shifted his weight, tightened his jaw. "And I appreciate it, but I think Yancey and the guys can handle it from now on."

"I helped build those stores, Angel."

"Store. You helped build the first one. Then you protested the second one. And, let's be honest here, Marcus, because I have very little else to lose at this point, you didn't see the sense of the first one. You were Johnny-come-lately on it."

He twisted his lips and bounced on his toes. "Yancey come running to you telling tales?"

"Yancey is a valued employee and near-partner." She paused, looked at him. "And I know you only too well."

"Yeah. I know you, too." This was about to get uglier than she was prepared for and Angel steadied herself. "Mark would have had his college degree and been well away from the plumbing business if you hadn't got knocked up first rattle out of the box."

"Well, it wasn't an immaculate conception, if that's what you're implying."

"I'm not implying nothing. I'm saying it. You were afraid you'd lose him to some fancy college girl who was better than you, so you got pregnant. And then when that wasn't enough you did it again and made sure he sacrificed what was left of his college days!"

He was leaning into her space. Angel gauged the distance to the phone. Yes, she could grab it, bean him with it, and then call for help.

"You've a short memory and poor eyesight indeed if you don't know what that framed diploma is on his office wall." She leaned toward him. "And back up, Marcus. Get out of my face, then get out of my stores!"

"You're an ungrateful, low-class bitch with an acid tongue. I told him that from the beginning." He pulled away and turned to leave, then spun back. "Just like your mother!"

He pulled the bedroom door open and said mother almost fell through. "Just proves my point!" he shot over his shoulder.

Delores balanced herself by hanging onto the doorknob. "Low class, my ass."

"Mother..."

93

"I'm going to show his low-class ass out the door!" And she'd followed.

Angel had picked up the phone to call Eric.

She looked over at him now. His chin rested in his upturned palm and he waited for her to begin. Another male waiting on her to do or say something. To finish or to start.

"Like I said, it was awful. We discussed genealogy and family history. We gave references." Eric's mouth was curving into a smile. "And I think it's safe to say, that Marcus O'Shea Sr. has left my building for the last time." She gave her head an abrupt nod. "Until he can't stand it and comes back."

He tried to control the laugh, but it bubbled up as a snort anyway. "You called him a bastard..."

"Not in so many words."

"And he..."

"Impugned my mother."

He didn't even try to hide the smile and she found a laugh escaping her throat. The last thing it was was funny, but Eric had helped put it in perspective. She watched him fight to sober his features and finally manage it. "Why is it," he began, "that the most stressful times bring out the worst possible sides of people?" He shook his head. "Or the best. But we seem to be stuck in worst mode with our families."

"I am going to consider it a cautionary tale well-learned."

He nodded. "But you're right. He will be back."

There was that. Angel knew whom she was up against. Little deterred the old man, who heard what he wanted to hear, threw insults, and let all the emotional fallout rain down unabated. "Undoubtedly. He'll chalk it up to post-traumatic stress on my part and weasel his way back in. Or die trying. Short of a restraining order, there's little I can do." She rubbed at the bruise which covered her left arm from wrist to shoulder. Amazing it wasn't broken was what the doctors said. Because it was covering my heart, which is broken, she wanted to answer them. "Of course, once I get back to the stores, even he will be able to sense the unwelcome sign."

"Or you could just put your mother on guard duty."

That was the problem with knowing each other for so long and of having their families in the general area: for the O'Sheas and the Eubanks there were few surprises in either's family.

Delores Buttons was a small town social-climber. She had been mortified when her college freshman daughter became pregnant by her long time boyfriend, the plumber's son. She had felt Angel, bright and popular, could do so much better in the university husband sweepstakes than a hometown boy who hadn't fallen far from the parental tree. Rather than be attached to a family she felt superior to--Henry Buttons' unsuccessful, barely-made-ends-meet insurance agency versus the O'Shea plumbing business's success notwithstanding--Delores tried to persuade Angel to not marry Mark, to give the baby up or have an abortion, to not "ruin her chances." Henry had remained silent on the subject, as he usually did when Delores held forth.

Marcus Sr.'s opinion was as obvious, and as heartfelt, as Delores's. Angel and Mark may have been the high school favorites, popular, scholastic cream of the crop, but she was a tramp, just like her older sister, who had made a run through the sports teams even he had heard about. He'd hoped the year of separation when Mark went to college would have been the end of the romance. But no, she trailed him there when she graduated high school, not content to put herself at the junior college where she belonged. That Angel had earned a full-ride scholarship seemed to elude him. That his son was not only willing but eager to marry the girl appalled him.

They struggled along through her freshman year and his sophomore, but the birth of Jason and then the pregnancy with Travis ended her career and severely curtailed his. A better man than Marcus would have steadied the youngsters financially, which is what the Buttons scraped and did. One look at the grandchild had been all it took to turn Delores into a grandmother of the first order. Even Iona, Mark's mother, long divorced from his father, would call and chastise the man. Just why was he upset with an honorable son and two precious grandsons? His answer to her did not bear repeating.

But even with the help from the Buttons, the young family hit hard times. Hat in hand, Mark asked his father for the job he'd had in high school and began the courses to be a master plumber. If it were his fate, he would be the best. Marcus, shamed by ex- and present wives, gave him the job and paid for the courses.

It took six years to complete his business degree, but by that time, Mark had options and ideas. Being a plumber, no matter the good income, held no appeal to him, but it would be foolish not to trade on what he knew, and O'Shea's Plumbing Supplies became a reality. He sold to the trade but did not restrict himself from the public. Angel worked beside him, making a playroom for the boys in a second office so she could do the bookkeeping into the evening hours, and the boys could go to sleep. She encouraged Mark to begin do-it-yourself, how to know when you're in trouble, and plumbing safety classes. They filled quickly. After struggling for so long, their success only seemed to be overnight. And then they did it all over again in a store thirty miles away.

"Mother on guard duty. That would keep her busy. Which is one of the reasons for my call." She pushed herself up in the chair, found her butt to sit on and not her backbone. "She's been a rock, but she has to go." He nodded. "Do you think Stella and Miguel's daughters could or would manage me? I'd pay them. Handsomely."

"Can't think why not. But how will you ease your mother out?"

"I'll have to make her mad. It works every time."

His gaze roved to the kitchen windows where they could see their mothers conferring. "What if we send them on a vacation together? A reward for being there for us."

"I wish we could talk them into taking our places in Cancun. *That's* paid for." And while something would certainly have to be done about it and soon, the words were out of her mouth before she thought about them. "Oh, Jesus, Eric, I'm sorry." Paulina, Mark, and she always enjoyed Cancun, the food, the sand, the night life, the freedom from responsibility. But Eric loved it. It answered the same call in him that was met by a new golf course for Mark. The merest suggestion that they try other venues always brought a frown and an 'if you insist.' Brochures for other places might show up at their winter doldrums planning dinner in January, but they were a tease.

"They'd never go that far so soon after."

So soon after. The words echoed in her mind. When would it not be *so soon after*? "True."

"But how about a spa? Not too far away. Where you and Paulina went last year..." His voice trailed off.

They had to stop stepping on each other's memories. It had been a fun long weekend, a fitting retaliation for one of the guys' golf adventures. It was a good memory, worthy of sharing, just like all the Cancuns.

She made herself brighten. "Brilliant. Absolutely brilliant. I'll put Travis to work on it." She patted her dress pocket and pulled her cell phone from it. One key later, she had him on the line and explained quickly what they needed, listened as he started Internet research. "We can tell them they can always be home in hours if we need them," she said to Eric before being pulled back by Travis's voice. She listened again. "Yes, that's it. Call back soon."

She closed the phone. "I smell freedom already." She watched their mothers through the French doors. The women were about to converge on them. "One more thing though." She twisted in her seat and sobered her features. "Yancey was concerned about the new business. The bank has already called about the loan." Eric's eyes narrowed. "I told him we were going ahead. I hope that was all right."

He was silent a moment, and she heard the footsteps of rapidly approaching mothers and the clink of ice in a pitcher. "Eric?"

"Of course." He brought himself back from some faraway place. "We have to go forward, Angel. Time doesn't care for our woes, and Yancey and Miguel have too much at stake for us not to."

"Good." She settled back in the chair and let Delores

and Melba freshen the tea, rearrange a tray of cookies, and in general, act as if nothing had happened to scar the lives of so many people. "Mother," she broke in on their chrysanthemum versus anemone conversation, a sham, no doubt for what they had really been discussing: their in-laws. It was Delores's new, favorite subject, having replaced reality TV. "Eric and I have a surprise for the two of you."

They stopped what they were doing and she could see them each hold their breath. What did they possibly think she was going to say? "Oh?" her mother asked.

"We thought you'd like a break from taking care of us, so Travis is arranging for the two of you to go to the spa in Austin where Paulina and I went last year."

"Oh, darling, that's not necessary." The words came out with her breath. Delores had her hand over her heart now and Melba had sat down.

Eric put in his two cents' worth. "Lots of things aren't necessary, but life's better when you do them. This is one. You're going."

Melba and Delores exchanged looks, I-told-you-so clearly written across both brows. "Of course, dear." Melba folded her hands and acquiesced without a whimper.

Delores was made of sterner stuff.

"And Iona? Where is she going?"

"Home. Her home," she added to her Delores's raised brow. "You know my track record today, Mother. What's one more O'Shea burned by my acid tongue?"

Chapter 10

Friday: One week later

Eric sifted through the landscape plans with his left hand, pulling the one he wanted from the bottom. He tried to keep the others on the dining table by trapping them with his right elbow. While one part of him was pleased to have his workspace so close to everything he needed--the kitchen, the bathroom, the TV--the other part was appalled at how quickly he'd rearranged his life, post-Paulina. Her number one dictum: work stayed at work, hence she did not bring hers home, although she might be midnight coming in, and his could very well stay in the backyard office. So landscape plans had not crept into the house. He'd rarely returned phone calls except from the backyard. Mark, whose backyard had often resembled a pipe fitter's assemblage as he'd tried to figure out a new way of doing an old task, had told Eric on more than one occasion that he was henpecked. Or words to that effect. Maybe so. But when he passed through his French doors and found his wife at home, business did not interfere with family.

Now, with his mother gone to Austin, there was no active female influence in the house. He cast a wary eye around the area he could see, from kitchen to den to informal dining. Melba was due back tomorrow. If he were to keep independence for himself and Ty, something and *some ones* were going to have to be whipped back into shape.

There was a stack of dishes in the sink, a big sin even in his book, and he'd caught Ty drinking from the orange juice carton this morning. Tuesday noon, Melba had left the laundry caught up and the beds clean, the house vacuumed and a completed stack of written, addressed, and stamped thank-yous for him to read, sign, and seal. They were still by his chair, and the terrazzo floor in the entry hall bore the marks of Ty's feet as he'd run in from the rain yesterday. He hadn't made his bed one-armed, and the washer was surrounded by towels and underwear. All this, in just three days.

Maybe they really couldn't make it on their own.

His only saving grace was he didn't physically hurt as he had a week ago. The soreness was dissipating, the bruises disappearing. His foot was straightening out and his right arm was just in a simple sling. Ty was still watchful, still hesitant to leave him alone. The boy surrounded himself with friends, bringing home peers Eric had only heard about and maybe never seen. William was always in the group. Did they seek friends to fill the void left by a parent?

With what was he to fill the void left by a spouse?

So while his physical injuries were improving, his mental and spiritual ones were roiling. Paulina's things were in the bathroom, her robe still on the back of the door. He'd touch them, decide to get a box, put them back. He couldn't do it yet. He couldn't erase her presence.

At times, she'd been overbearing, manipulative, sharp-tongued.

Wry, witty, sardonic, pull-no-punches-this-is-how-it-is. Impulsive just often enough that he didn't know what to expect. Despite their exchange at the club two weeks ago, he loved her--and knew she no longer loved him. Not like she used to. Not like he wanted her to. Not like she should have.

He shot a glance at the kitchen calendar, the days of this week marked out in red, CANCUN blazoned across them. He loved Cancun because Paulina came closest to being her old self there. She relaxed and shed the office-boss pretensions. She became just his wife. Except for his loss of the argument about another child, he always came home a winner from Cancun and he couldn't imagine going elsewhere.

But this is where he was now, in a disheveled house of his own making.

He spoke everyday with Angel. Stella and Miguel's daughters had been delighted to split the job of Angel-care around summer school and jobs. Did Delores think this was just temporary while she was away? He might have to face his mother on the housekeeping issue, but even that would be preferred to Angel facing Delores on the issue of independence. The girls drove Angel to the doctor, and she'd ventured to the O'Shea stores. As Miguel had informed him on their tour of landscape jobs this morning, Marcus had yet to show his face. What, his foreman had asked, had Angel said to the old man? He needed the words for his mother-in-law.

Eric had laughed at that and shared nothing.

Now voices raised in shrill cries reached his ears from the backyard. He swiveled to see that the male pack of five, who had been embroiled in a rather rough game of Marco Polo, had been invaded by six young women clad in--virtually nothing. What were their mothers thinking? But swimming didn't seem to be on their minds--skimpy attire was bad enough, but wet, skimpy attire would be worse--as they all settled on the edge of the pool and put their feet in the water. The game of Marco Polo came to an abrupt halt, and the boys scrambled to bring them drinks and not act as dorky as Eric could remember himself feeling.

But he'd done this socializing at the public pool, not the privacy of a backyard. Ty had been told he could never have pool guests without an adult at home. But the adult in residence was cripped up and useless. He was seriously out of his league with this group of boys vs. group of girls scenario. No doubt Paulina would have known how to diffuse it, not that Ty would have spoken to her for a month. Now a hotbed of female squeals and male braggadocio, his backyard was ripe for a situation to get out of hand, and if it were bad now, what would another year or two bring?

He sighed and sank into a dining chair. Ruffles, who had appeared from out of nowhere, jumped into his lap and made a bed. Usually, Ty spent his summers, when not in one sport camp or another, with Eric on the job. As he'd physically matured, he'd progressed from simple fetching from the back of the truck to working with the crews. He didn't particularly like it, but Eric would hazard that Ty was the only boy in school who knew what was wrong with the bushes in the junior high landscaping. *You don't have to follow in my footsteps,* Eric had told him once after a particularly scowl-filled exchange, *but you do have to learn what puts food on your table.* Ty had arched a brow ala his mother. *Mom pays the taxes,* Eric had retorted, *and I know you'd rather eat than pay taxes.* That had earned an eye roll, but the discussion had ended. However, these last two weeks chaos had reigned and all that had gone to hell. It was time both he and Ty went back to work on a steady basis.

They could begin with the kitchen and laundry just as soon as everyone's mother called them home to supper and the impromptu party ended. In the meantime, vigilance was the price he would have to pay.

***

"You sure you don't want me to start supper, Angel?" Joanie Cruz gave the granite counters a final swipe and hung the dish towel on the oven door. "It's not a problem, I swear." She rested her hands on her hips and fixed Angel with a look that defied her to protest.

"You are not hired to cook, Joanie. Scoot! Go on your date!"

"Don't have a date tonight." Joanie leaned across the bar and thrummed her fingers toward Angel who sat at the breakfast table, her feet elevated on a chair and her back propped with a sofa pillow. The laptop hummed in front of her, displaying the week's receipts. "Aren't Travis and Jason coming home? Aren't you going to feed them?"

Ah. That explained the sudden domesticity. "How old are you?"

"Nineteen in August. And I'm a second semester sophomore. Just ask mama."

Ambitious. Going places. Looking to secure her future. "I believe you, honey. You're a smart girl. But the boys are too old for you."

"Annn-gelll..." the girl made her name into a groan. "Let me decide that. There aren't any girlfriends, are there? Fiancées?"

"Not that I know of, but girlfriends might have a tendency to disappear in times of family trouble."

"Not if they're in it for the long haul."

Angel chuckled. "Touché. What is your daddy going to think about you scoping out my guys who are already out of college?" She squinted her eyes. "Five years and six--almost seven--years older than you?"

"He's going to want me to go for the med student, but I think I'll settle for the computer nerd."

"Don't ever settle, Joanie."

She flushed. "I didn't mean..."

Angel smiled at her. "I know what you meant." She closed the computer. All the numbers were giving her a headache. "They're supposed to be bringing groceries from some fancy store."

"And who's going to cook them?" Joanie stuck her lip out and faked a pout. "You?"

"The guys haven't starved living on their own."

Now Joanie sniffed. Only a young woman confident in herself--and her employer--would pull such a stunt. She'd known Jason and Travis since they were in junior high and she in elementary, had babysat William. Funny, Angel had never put her together romantically with either of her older sons, but it was an intriguing thought. Joanie was a live wire. Angel didn't know if the young men in question were up to the challenge.

"Why don't you call your older sister and see if she wants to come over, too." She smiled her best catty smile. "I might as well marry them both off at once."

Joanie narrowed her eyes. "Luce has a boyfriend. They're serious."

"So no competition allowed."

"None." She snapped to attention, her dark ponytail bouncing around her shoulders and her brown eyes flashing. "But if you can manage for an hour, I need to go home and change," she was already pulling her car keys from her purse, "and I'm off the clock tonight, okay? I'm just doing this as a favor to you and yours." She stood by the door. "Need anything before I go? Bathroom? Water? Plumper pillow? You got both phones? You call if you need me back quick."

"I'm fine. Go on, Joanie. And damn straight you're off the clock," she called to the girl's back as she skipped out the sliding door to the patio.

Angel sighed and leaned her head back to rest it on the breakfast nook wall. She closed her eyes and was amazed by the sound of... silence. She was alone in the house. Alone for the first time in how long?

Two weeks. Two weeks ago just before Mark came in with the Jag. She'd come back from the club after decorating. She'd fixed herself a glass of limeade and sat at this table and pulled her list of to-dos for Mark's surprise party the next day from its hiding place in the china cabinet. She reread the list and noted there was nothing that needed doing until he was out of the way, and the next day's golf tournament was going to take care of that. She'd stopped by the bar, added a dash of vodka to the limeade, and gone upstairs to shower. She'd been alone in the house until Mark had come home and then William.

She was alone again, but it was different this time. This aloneness brought a dull spiritual ache. This wasn't going to be cured by a house full of sons trying to shove their own grief under a happy façade in order to make their mother feel better. This ache would be cured by nothing but time.

Or so she had been told.

Reverend Johns had left a book for her to read. Delores had talked about widows she'd known who had lived very fulfilling lives 'afterward.' Melba had given her a squeeze and told her to call any time. That was the one resource whose advice might actually be useful.

Angel's reverie was broken by the click of nails on the tile from the den. She cracked open an eye and watched Dweeb enter the room. He stopped to sniff Mark's chair and then came to her, laying his large head in her lap and settling his rump as close to her chair as possible. She scratched his ears and rubbed his neck. "Why aren't you with William? Joanie'll have a fit if she finds you in the house." The girl, for all her protestations of not doing housework, had spent the early afternoon straightening up the downstairs unasked and shooing the retriever from room to room. She finally declared him canine *non grata* and escorted him out the back door. "Not going to tell me how you snuck past Joanie?" He rolled his eyes at her.

"I need to learn to sneak past Joanie," she continued. "Hell, I want to sneak past myself. I want to go somewhere else. Be someone else, dog." He whimpered.

"Yeah, you and me both." She pulled her feet out of the other chair and straightened up. Dweeb stayed underfoot as she balanced herself to a stand and limped to the kitchen. She was steadier than last week and had managed to get on real clothes the last two days. "I'm not supposed to be here, you know. I'm supposed to be on the beach ogling overweight Europeans." She rounded the counter into the kitchen and opened the refrigerator. The dog settled by his food bowl. "You know what we need around here, Dweeb? Besides a good stiff drink and big bowl of ice cream? We need some laughter." She pulled out the orange juice carton and turned to find a glass in the dish drainer. "Let's have a party. The boys are shopping, Joanie's cooking, and I'm too weak to clean up. Sounds like an idea whose time has come." She toasted the dog, who tilted his head from side to side. "Let's call Eric and Ty and see if they have anything on their social calendar. What say?"

Dweeb barked, just like the boys had taught him to do.

***

Angel planned for the guys to pull apart the formal dining table and add the leaf. As the only females present, she'd have Joanie sit at the end near the kitchen as cook and hostess and she'd take Mark's spot. They'd have a semi-formal dinner of spaghetti, or whatever the boys brought.

It didn't work that way. Following Jason and Travis through the patio door were two young ladies Angel didn't know. She was curious. Joanie was narrow-eyed and couldn't wait to whisper, "I told you so. In it for the long haul?" The jealousy didn't suit the heretofore sweet-natured girl--and she was just eighteen--but Angel wondered the same thing. For all the looks and touches between her sons and these young women, just how long had they known them and where had they been?

"California." The blonde was tall and leggy, taller

than Jason, the son she was following.

"We had to go see our dad. He was getting married for the *n*th time." The redhead, the one attracted to Angel's home-grown computer nerd.

"We are so sorry to hear about your husband."

Fraternal twins. Lori and Reagan. ("Daddy had some sort of Republican thing going on.") A month ago, her sons had found sisters in the senior nursing class, found them in a bar on Dallas' Lower Greenville if their hasty, sweep-the-details-under-the-rug story was to be believed. Then they'd waited to bring them home to meet her until some time had passed, both for their relationships and for their grief.

Joanie had been outsmarted. It remained to be seen if she'd also been outclassed.

"Hey, Joanie, out of high school yet?" Jason didn't wait for her answer as he carried two cases of beer through the kitchen to the second refrigerator in the utility room. So much for them not planning on staying the weekend. And the girls? she wanted to ask. Where were they staying?

As if Lori, the blonde, could read her mind, "We've got to scoot back tonight. We're both working this weekend."

"Oh, what a wonderful dog!" Dweeb had discovered Reagan, the redhead. R the r. That's how she'd remember them until and if they became more permanent fixtures. Dweeb, it was obvious, would remember the difference by smell.

Angel shot Travis a look and he grabbed Dweeb by the collar, opened the patio door and pushed him out. Once over his astonishment at having been ousted, the dog glued his nose to the glass and whimpered.

"Mother, you have spoiled that dog."

"Talk to your da--brother."

A pause so tiny as to be insignificant. Except they all felt it. Mark had been the great spoiler.

Jason jumped in. "Where is the wonder kid?"

"At the Eubanks'. Waiting for one of you to run over there and fetch them for dinner. Eric and Ty are joining us."

"I told you we should have bought more sausage," Jason scolded his brother. "If we run out, Mom, it's not my fault."

"There's plenty in the freezer. If I don't have enough cash..."

"Mom! Our treat," Travis rushed to say. "Anyway, wait until you taste it. You may not be so anxious to share the cost then."

"Fair enough. Who's going to get Eric?"

"I will, Angel." Joanie untied her apron. She'd come back looking ready for a date, but now she picked up her purse and leaned over to whisper. "I think you have enough help. Okay I see you in the morning?"

"You're a sweetheart." Angel kissed her on the cheek.

And a class act.

**

Three hours later, the dishes were cleared. It had taken Jason, Travis and the girls almost two hours to do the outside cooking what with all the attendant squealing and nonsense. Steaks, sausage, grilled asparagus and red peppers, a salad that appeared from a bag and a cheesecake from a box... yes, it was a male-affair all the way and Angel noted that both she and Eric cleaned their plates.

The older brothers had tried to dupe the younger boys into doing the clean-up but the girls had rescued them. Maybe there was potential there. At least, someone had raised them right as far as she could see.

So she and Eric faced each other down the length of the dining table. The boys were teasing Dweeb with a series of 'what says' and from all the dish sounds coming from the kitchen, she was glad they'd used the everyday. Paper might have been preferable.

"Have you heard from your mom?" Eric lifted the wine glass for a final sip.

Angel pulled her cell phone from her pocket and studied the crystal. "Not since right before you got here."

He quirked a brow.

"She approved the guest list, pooh-poohed the lack of fruit in the menu, and said bad things to Jason when I passed him the phone, all of which had to do with not getting to meet Lori and Reagan." She tipped her water glass to her lips.

"They can't be home soon enough."

She almost spurted her water. "How do you plan on handling yours?"

"She's going to have a shit-fit when she sees the house unless I can rouse some enthusiasm for clean from the boy."

"Give him the ultimatum: clean or grandmother."

"Don't dare do that. He likes her and loves her cooking."

"Why don't you hire Luce for the morning? She can have it clean before he gets up."

"I like the way you think, Mrs. O'Shea."

The name hung there. Well, that's who she was, even if there were no longer a Mr. O'Shea. Socially, she was Mrs. Mark O'Shea. She'd even signed their first checking account checks that way before bending to Paulina's advice, getting her own account and signing as Angel B. O'Shea. Good long term advice, as it turned out.

"Angel?"

Eric's voice broke her reverie. "Sorry. I got stuck on my name." She bit her lip and switched to wine. "I'm still Mrs. O'Shea."

"Angel..."

"Eric, I'm being foolish. Silly. I don't mean to spoil our lovely meal. Just a quirk."

He smiled. "Don't apologize to me. I'm the one who still needs his mother."

"Let her stay a week?"

"And tell her good-bye when? Never?"

"When..." Dare she say? Tears welled up. "When you heal. When you find... when life goes on."

"When I find someone else?" He cut to the chase. "Are you going to find someone else?"

"Didn't you ever discuss it, you and Paulina? That if something happened to one of you, the other should remarry?"

He drew his brows together. "Some. I thought it would be me. Hit by a bulldozer." He paused, as if couching his next words. "You? Surely you'll find someone?"

"Trust me, Eric, you are a much better catch than a woman in her mid-forties with a teenage son."

"That would be a financially independent woman."

"With debts."

"And going businesses."

"And the only person who would consider me a trophy wife is," she did a quick calculation in her mind, "seventy-six."

"And you can do arithmetic in your head. What a catch!"

That made her laugh. "With my luck, he'd live to be ninety-six and use up all his funds on pretty nurses."

"Then you'd be sixty-five and I'd look good to you."

Silence. Off her guard. Shut down. No breath.

"Mom," William burst through the swinging door into the kitchen, "Lori wants..." he stopped, mouth half-open, eyes darting from one to the other.

My God, how stunned did the two of them look if William was picking up on it? "What, sweetie?" She tore her eyes from Eric's reddening face. "What does Lori want?"

He crinkled his forehead. "Are you okay?"

"Yes, William." He had become as sensitive as the latest weather radar. "Eric and I were having a serious discussion."

"Then you need to lighten up." He gave a shiver. "Lori wants to know if you want coffee. But she only found decaf."

"Decaf would be great. And the real is... you know where it is, William. Show her." She was a bit sharp with him, and he seemed grateful to leave.

She pivoted back to Eric. "I think I need more sleep."

"I know what you mean."

"Eric..."

"Angel, we've been friends since before the boys were born. We shouldn't have to watch our words."

Why had his remark upset her so? he wondered. It

wasn't like it was a proposal or even a suggestion. It was... it was two weeks after the death of his wife and his best friend. That was the problem. He was scrambling--scrambling like Dweeb on wet tile--to gain a foothold in order to get his life back together, and he did not even have the comfort of a best friend to help him. Had just one spouse of the four died, it would have been easier, there would have been two of them to help the one remaining. But that wasn't the way it had played out. They were one on one, he and Angel, one on one without their other halves and best friends. Lost.

They knew each other and knew each other well, but there were holes where once there had been Mark and Paulina. Holes that gaped and made the two of them awkward with each other. It wasn't right, and it was damn sure inconvenient, and furthermore, he wasn't sure what to do about it.

"Time," she announced.

"Time for what?" To go? She was asking them to leave?

"We need time, Eric. Time to straighten everything out in our minds. To get our houses in order." She shook her head. "And then I wonder if there'll ever be enough time. I met with the lawyers yesterday. Even though Mark and I thought we had it laid out so neatly, there's such an amount of work to do. Probate. Putting everything in just my name. Insurance claims for the car and the hospital. I'm," she paused, searching for the right word, "overwhelmed."

He could relate. "Travis and Jason?" Older sons, grown, up-and-coming responsible members of society. An option he didn't have.

"Would do anything I asked of them. And what I'm

asking is for them to work and stay in school. I need to know they're having a normal life."

There was female laughter from the kitchen. "I'd say they were trying."

She shot him a wry look. "They're torn…"

"They're afraid, Angel. They'll do anything you ask and you know it. Just give the lawyer his fee and leave him to it."

That brought a smile. "Is that what you're doing?"

"Damn straight." He shifted in his chair, twisting to rub his leg and knee. "I've got too many ditches to dig to worry about high-falutin' legalese."

"Said from the safety of being--having been--married to a lawyer."

He let the change of tense wash over him. "If nothing else, I learned when to turn it over."

"Oh, Eric." Desperation slipped into her voice as she studied the wooden blinds just past his head, her eyes unfocused. "What are we going to do? How?"

"One thing at a time, Ange. One step. One lawyer. One," he changed his next words as a crash came from the kitchen followed by Dweeb's barking and a female cry of 'the coffee!', "catastrophe at a time."

"Oh." She turned to the swinging door, anticipating its movement. "Family life at its best. Just one snafu after another."

"Mom," William called as he and Ty were through the door first, "we didn't do it. At least not all of it." They had Dweeb by the collar. It took both of them to drag the dog to the den. Eric heard the patio door open and a 'woof!' as Dweeb was expelled. The boys returned to the table and took their places where they'd been during dinner. They folded their hands in their laps and looked guilty as sin.

But, Eric thought, they made a nice family picture, even with the two boys shooting desperate looks at each other that belied William's statement of semi-innocence. The whisk of a broom was heard in the kitchen and water started in the sink. Lori popped her head through the door with a "it'll be just another minute" and silence settled.

"You can find them online, you know." William cast a look at her out of the corner of his eye. "Jason said he'd find them."

"I can buy them at the department store."

"Even better."

"Boys…"

"I love you, Mom."

So scared, Eric thought. So scared to lose his mother a thirteen-year-old boy didn't mind saying those words in front of his best friend, the guy most guaranteed to not let you forget you ever uttered them.

"I know, sweetheart," she answered him. "Maybe we'll use this as an excuse to get another pattern."

"Start over?"

"Yeah." She reached and patted his hand. "We'll be doing a lot of that."

Fate's Second Decision
Angel and Paulina

Prologue
Sarah Neely

Sarah stared at the cell phone in her trembling hand. *Think, Sarah, think*, she admonished herself. *Did she dial 911 and risk getting an operator in Peoria or was there a special code? Peoria? Where the* hell *was her mind to think of that? Didn't she store in memory a special code for the highway patrol?*

She moved around to the front of their car, used the headlights as a shield against the night. Adam's back had just disappeared through the broken guardrail, and she could hear him crashing through the shrubs on his descent toward the river. He might be the one doing the investigating, but it had been her quick eyes which had seen the accident area in time to get him to pull over and stop instead of becoming part of it. An object in the road, a deer from the shape and size, skid marks, a broken rail... didn't really take a genius to figure this out.

She continued searching her stored numbers. Why hadn't she put a blank in front of it, like she had the 'in case of emergency' number? Why did she have to be so alphabetical? Wasn't the phone number on the back of her driver's license? Hell--she could have just turned *it* over! But the number appeared on the cell phone face and she pushed 'send.'

A voice answered, asked her name, her situation, then

offered help.

"I'm Sarah Neely and… and there's been an accident. North of the Timber Bridge. You know, near…" hell, where did she live? "…near Fleming."

"Are you hurt, Sarah?"

"No."

"Is anyone hurt?"

"Probably. My husband went to check. The guardrail is broken and there are skid marks. Maybe there's a car in the river?" She needed to account for all possibilities, didn't she? The disembodied voice on the other end needed to take her seriously, to understand that Sarah Neely was in the midst of a crisis.

"Were you in the accident, Sarah?"

"No."

"Do you see the other car?"

"No." What was this lady's problem? Couldn't she tell someone needed help? "Can't you come? Can't you send somebody?"

"I've got a patrolman on the way now." *Thank God!* "Where is your husband?"

Hadn't she already said? But there was Adam now, limping toward her, his head downcast. "He's here."

"Is he okay?"

"Yes." And for a reason she'd never know, Sarah closed the cell phone on the dispatcher and held out her arms to Adam. "Are you hurt?"

He ignored her question. "It's a Jag," he said as he squeezed her, then grasped her upper arms and held her from him. "It's Mark's."

She couldn't cry. She had to hold herself together for the officer when he arrived. She had to point the way down the slope. She had to be brave for Adam, even as she didn't really want to know what he'd found. He was the one limping and yet he helped her around the car and into the front seat. But that was Adam. He went to the trunk and got the blanket they kept there. Sarah sat stunned and watched him struggle with it, even as the patrol car whipped to a stop beside them and a young man, all business and bustle, got out.

It's Mark's. But that didn't happen. Friends you'd just laughed with and talked to and eaten dinner with--it didn't happen, did it? That they walked out the door and got into a car and then were no more?

Chapter 11

Monday noon
Three days after the accident

Dweeb was sitting on her head. That had to be it, Angel thought. Nothing else could possibly explain the weight there. And she couldn't move. It hurt to breathe. Her eyes wouldn't open. Only Dweeb where he shouldn't be. Why had Mark let him in the bedroom?

And why wasn't he turning off that infernal alarm? *Beep, beep, beep.* Her alarm didn't sound like that, irritating, speeding up, adding a squeak. Her alarm would wake the dead, not annoy them.

Something touched her right hand, smoothed the top of it, curled her fingers around their own. Someone was holding her hand and it wasn't Dweeb and his paw.

Nor was it Mark. Hand holding, even as foreplay, was not in his vocabulary. The last hand Mark had held would have been William's and the boy a toddler.

"Angel."

A whisper. She felt breath on the back of her hand, a squeeze.

"Angel, wake up." Her hand was shaken, just a little.

The voice was familiar. Female. Someone she'd

heard whisper before.

"C'mon, Angel. For me."

Whoever *me* was.

She turned her head toward the voice, felt Dweeb shift and not in a pleasant way, not as in getting off the bed. She forced her eyelids to open, felt them flutter closed. "Pauli--," she said in an exhaled breath. She used all her air just to say that.

"Yes. Me. C'mon, Angel, wake up." Now her hand was squeezed more tightly and Paulina moved her little shakes to Angel's arm. "No fair sleeping when I can't. Wake up." Shake. Squeeze. "Wake up and I promise not to find your mother for another hour."

What did her mother have to do with this? She was thinking more clearly than she was talking because all she could manage was a pitiful "Wha--?" But she forced her eyes open, made them focus.

Paulina was sitting beside her bed. She had a black right eye and a cut above it. No make-up. As if all the other evidence were not enough, the fact that Paulina had no make-up was enough for Angel to know something was very wrong. She wore a tee shirt, a wrinkled tee shirt.

Oh God, Angel thought. *Oh God oh God oh God.* Paulina was never wrinkled.

She took a deep breath and rushed the words. "What's wrong, Pauli?" She used Mark's nickname for her friend. It seemed to be right. And it was shorter, took less breath, less concentration.

"Look around. Tell me where you are."

Paulina didn't know? And... look around? She couldn't breathe and she was supposed to *look around*? But, moving her head, Angel cast her eyes up and back.

The evidence mounted. A TV on the wall. Flowers. Single bed. Rails. IVs in her left arm. The non-stop beeping from a machine at her left shoulder.

Her throat closed and her voice choked. "What happened?" She started to panic, felt the rising of the blood in her face, heard the beeping speed up.

"We were in an accident. A bad one." Paulina stood and leaned over the bed. She grasped Angel's upper arms and pulled her to focus on Paulina. "Friday night. After the dance. Do you remember the deer?"

Angel drew her brows together as if doing so would improve her understanding. "I think so."

"Well, we hit one of them." She paused. "I hit one of them." She rushed her next words. "And I couldn't control the car and Mark couldn't either and we went over the embankment and into the river."

Angel turned her mind's-eye to the memory. Shouting. Panic. Fear. Eric grabbing her but the force of the plunge pulling her from his hands. The seatbelt clenching and the air bags exploding and turning over and over...

The room door was shoved open and two strangers in scrubs hurriedly entered. Paulina moved away from the bed as the man and woman made a fuss over the machine, pulled on Angel's eyelids and had her look left and right. Her toes were touched, her fingertips. They adjusted the weight on her head.

"Angel," the woman said, "Angel, calm down. That sound is the heart monitor and you've got it galloping."

Like she cared. Couldn't it take it? The vicious mother streak rose in her, the one that Jason and Travis said was the real Angel, the mother bear guarding her cubs and taking no prisoners. "Who are you? Get away from me!"

"Angel, I'm Dr. Cavanaugh and this is John." Her low, soothing voice indicated the man beside her. *Calm down*, the voice said without saying so. *Don't make me make you calm down.* Her eyes didn't leave Angel's. "You were in an accident and now you're at Parkland Hospital. We're going to take good care of you so those boys of yours can stop harassing my staff with questions about when you can go home. And your med student is the worst one."

The boys. And of course Jason would be the worst. He would have the most to fear. "Pauli?" It hurt, but Angel turned her head to her friend. "Where are the boys?"

"I'll get them in a minute."

"Pa--"

"In a minute." It wasn't quite Paulina's come-to-Jesus voice, but it was close. And Paulina was no fan of Jesus.

Angel watched as Paulina exchanged looks with the doctor and nurse. Dark, intense looks that she couldn't quite read, but which made her wary. "If she's okay for the minute, if it's okay with you, I'll stay and, ah, and we'll talk." Paulina shifted her weight, crossed her arms and folded her hands under them.

No make-up. Wrinkled tee. Old jeans. Nervous as a cat. Angel took a steadying breath. And another. She would make her heart slow down, she would make the monitor behave. She found herself praying, praying the doctor and nurse would stay and Paulina wouldn't talk to her. She didn't want to know what Paulina was going to say.

Because it had to be bad. If it wasn't, Mark would be

here. She had to stop Paulina from saying it.

"You're sure?" Dr. Cavanaugh asked Paulina.

She nodded.

"Then we'll be just down the hall. If this monitor gets to racing again…" She let the word linger, and then with the silence of soft-soled shoes, they were gone.

They studied each other as Paulina crossed back to the bed. She leaned forward and her fingers curled into the sheeting as if she could hang on for dear life. She bit at her lips.

"I don't want to know."

"I don't want to tell you."

Angel felt tears ease from her eyes. Paulina released her death grip on the sheet and wiped them away with her thumb. "It's bad all the way around, my friend."

Friend. More like sister. Certainly more of a sister than her own were. Being middle child really was a difficult position and a situation she had hoped to avoid with her own family. Three sons later, it was obvious that hadn't worked, and she wasn't willing to have a fourth to clear up the issue. Mark and she were the embodiment of the old wives' tale that to become pregnant, you had merely to wash your underwear together. She hoped the ten plus years between her families would serve to lessen middle-child syndrome for Travis. Ironically, the pregnancy with William was the reason she knew Paulina at all.

For three monthly appointments she had sat in the obstetrician's waiting room and noticed the tall, statuesque woman obviously on the same schedule as she. She wore business attire, not a hair out of place. Even as she morphed into maternity clothes, she was the picture of style. Angel felt like a frump, wearing Mark's tee shirts to cover the jeans she was sliding steadily down her abdomen. It wasn't a question of money--well, it was, but she swore it wasn't--that made her look like a woman who didn't care for her appearance, but of practicality. Why spend money they needed for the stores and the two sons at home on clothing she'd not have a use for by the next season? Even had she thought she'd have a third child, she'd not have saved her clothes from Travis and Jason: that wardrobe had been borrowed from friends and culled from Goodwill. She had been tempted to burn it. But for this last pregnancy--yes, it is, Mark, she'd told him--she'd allowed herself one nice outfit for church, two pairs of modestly priced slacks and tops for when she had to be in public at the store and good maternity underwear. Other than that, she would make do. So the stranger across from her, the woman with the cell phone peeking out of her leather briefcase and the perfect makeup, that woman intimidated Angel.

She was late for her six-month appointment and the waiting room was full, the doctor being held up on a delivery and everyone being asked to wait. There was but one seat left, next to this perfect stranger. She sat with legs crossed--Angel could no longer do that--swinging an expensive pump from her polished toes. She wasn't reading as she usually did, just staring off into space. Even sitting beside her seemed an invasion of her privacy, but Angel hadn't a choice. She sat.

"Your first?" The stranger quit her swing-routine and twisted in her chair.

Did she mean her? Angel looked up from her pocket calendar--somehow she had to get Travis to Scouts and Jason to baseball, events on opposite sides of town but which started at the same time. It didn't look like she would do either since the doctor was running late. She needed to call Mark.

Angel looked over her shoulder. The stranger did indeed mean her. "Oh, no. Third. Another boy." Angel glanced back at the calendar and then at her watch. "Have you been waiting long?"

"An hour."

Where were her manners? "Your first?" She was a bit on the old side for it to be a first, but she reeked of career woman, not someone knocked up her freshman year in college.

"Yes. A boy."

She wasn't jumping up and down about it, so Angel let the subject go and glanced again at her watch.

"Do you have another place to be?" the woman asked.

"The joys of three. A tight schedule and I need to call my husband. See if he can get them where they need to be." She started to rise. "I'll see if I can use the office phone."

"No. Don't bother." She reached into her briefcase and handed Angel her cell phone. "Use this. You won't lose your seat." She smiled.

Angel eased back down. "I need to get one of these," she explained as she punched in the store's number and ended up running the gauntlet to get to Mark. He griped and growled but agreed to pick the boys up from school and deliver them.

"Thank you," Angel said as she handed the phone back. "You'd think he hadn't a hand in them."

"Or some other part of his anatomy."

In hindsight, it was a risky remark, Angel thought. What if she hadn't laughed? What if she had been embarrassed? But she wasn't. They introduced themselves, found they lived in the same general neighborhood, and that Eubanks Landscaping was a major customer of O'Shea Plumbing. *Major* customer. Angel knew. She did the books. Could all these OB-waiting-room hours be construed as tax-deductible, time spent schmoozing a customer? The improbable thought cheered her even as the doctor arrived back. He stuck his head through the door that led from the waiting room into the inner sanctum and announced brightly: "Twins!"

"As if that justifies it all." Paulina smirked and then her name had been called and she had launched from the chair like a Roman candle.

After their next appointment, they went for coffee. As their friendship deepened, Angel began to think that by knowing her, Paulina had been a better mother than she had intended to be. It was what sisters did, being examples, lifting each other up. At least in theory, in Angel's idealized family world, because in practice her sisters were neither uplifting nor good examples. They were jealous, and Mark was ever anxious to point that little fact out to her.

But now, in this impersonal hospital world, she was the one being selfish. Eric would be here with Paulina if he could be.

"I don't suppose Eric... Mark... are in the next room?" Her throat constricted and shut down at 'room.'

"No." Paulina wiped her own tears.

"Real bad." A whispered croak. "Tell me." *Get it over with and tell me.*

"We hit the deer. The car flipped down the embankment and into the river. Landed on the passenger side. They, ah, they were, ah..." Paulina broke into sobs and her knees buckled. She caught herself before she collapsed onto the bed and Angel. Instead she cried into the edge of the sheet and Angel curled her fingers into her friend's hair even as her own tears snaked down her cheeks and into her ears and the corners of her mouth.

Mark couldn't be dead. Eric couldn't be dead. You didn't have plans for the rest of your life--hell, even for next week--and then they were nothing. Mark's birthday party, Cancun, seeing the boys married. So many things rushed through Angel's mind, backed up and bunched together that she had no coherent thoughts. All she could do was listen to her friend's sobs and know that these were Paulina's first tears over this. Angel had never seen her cry, not even well up at a schmaltzy movie. Paulina's tears had been reserved for laughing so hard she could cry, and even that wasn't often. Now they weren't so much comforting each other as bearing witness to each other's sorrow.

The door cracked open. Jason, Travis, William, and Ty stood in silent tableau. "Boys," was all Angel could get out until her tears broke into a torrent and then she and Paulina were surrounded and held and loved.

***

There was a downside to having one couple be your closest friends to the exclusion of any others. The Eubanks were close to no one but the O'Sheas, and in a crisis of this magnitude, Paulina had been alone Saturday morning in the ER cubicle until Sarah Neely bullied her way in. It briefly crossed Paulina's mind that she should offer Sarah a job as her front office receptionist. Anyone who could successfully get past the ER nurse's station could also keep out the unwanted in a brokerage firm.

She would think about it.

"What time is it?" she had asked.

"Just past five."

Sarah had stood at the foot of the bed and twisted her hands, then screwed her courage back together and looked Paulina in the eye. "Adam has called Reverend Johns and together they hope to beat anyone else to your house. I heard Angel tell someone tonight that that's where Ty and William were."

Oh, God. Ty. He shouldn't hear this from a stranger. Johns was the O'Shea preacher. "Couldn't he have called my parents instead?"

"It's all a confusion, Paulina. He did what he thought was best. Ministers know how to deliver this news. Better him than the highway patrol knocking on your door at two in the morning. And we didn't think of your parents. And we don't have the numbers..." Her voice trailed off. "I'm sorry. We should have thought more. He just didn't want the boys to be alone. And he didn't want some well-meaning club member..."

God, her head hurt. "It's okay, Sarah. Really. Thank you for taking charge and doing something."

Her right eye throbbed. The cut above it would have already been sutured had it been elsewhere on her body and not on her face. The plastic surgery resident was on his way.

Normally, a resident--a *trainee*, if you will--would not have done for Paulina, but under the circumstances, she didn't deserve better.

Eric was dead. Mark was dead. They wouldn't tell her about Angel, just hustled her off, separated them as soon as they had touched down in Dallas. The fact that she was in Dallas at all and not at the local hospital spoke for the confusion and urgency of the situation. So she was left with questions and uncertainties and Sarah Neely.

"What do you know about Angel?"

"All they'll say is she's in surgery." Sarah looked over her shoulder and then eased along the side of the bed to stand by Paulina's shoulder. She leaned down to whisper. "The highway patrol can hardly wait to get in here and question you."

"I'm sure they've filled multiple little vials with my blood to prove whether or not I was drinking." She rubbed at her arm. "I wasn't, Sarah."

"Lord, honey, I know that. They don't, but I do." A smile quirked the side of her mouth. "Old Standifer and I rode down together. He said he'd better nip it in the bud quick that he hadn't served you any alcohol and you didn't drink none anyway. That's quoting him." She gave a smug smile.

"You and Standifer?" That must have been an interesting ninety minutes in the car. Adam gone to get the Reverend, and Sarah and Standifer racing to the hospital to catch the officers. Paulina looked at Sarah and finally registered that she was still in her party dress. Shame filled her: Sarah hadn't come on this middle-of-the-night mission as a sycophant but because she thought herself Angel and Paulina's friend.

She wasn't. And Paulina didn't deserve such even if she was.

Tears threatened. She had rolled into and out of consciousness enough to know about Eric and Mark long before they landed. Once they pulled her from the wreckage, they wouldn't let her go back to sleep, told her she might have a concussion. So she'd had to be with that knowledge, had had to be awake, had heard every thwack of the chopper blades, every beep of the machine hooked to Angel. To know she had survived with minor injuries except the cut and knot on her head. Why had they bothered to put her in the chopper and not send her in an ambulance? Was it the possible alcohol issue? The question nagged at her. It was a burden Sarah Neely was doing nothing to assuage, no matter her good intentions.

"Has anyone called Eric's family?"

"Not that I know of. Unless Reverend Johns and Adam got Ty to give them the numbers."

But it was what she should do. "Is my purse here?"

Sarah nodded and retrieved it from the bedside table. "I'm sure they wanted your insurance card." She dug in it. "You want your cell phone." She held it out to Paulina.

She stared at it, at the lifeline to so many business associates, so few family members. "I can't see the names, Sarah. Scroll for Ellen Eubanks. Eric's older sister."

Sarah nodded her approval at the choice. "Got her."

"Hit the green button and let me have it."

Sarah helped her balance it to her ear, then turned to leave. "I'll be outside if you need me. Just ask for your Aunt Sarah."

"Thank you, Sarah."

She didn't cry then, telling Ellen. It hadn't been easy to find the words in the pre-dawn call, to say Melba's baby boy was gone and she'd been driving. Between sobs, Ellen had agreed to call Melba and Evie. She herself would arrive to be with Ty as soon as she could pull herself together, most likely before noon.

131

Paulina had ended the call and shuddered. She hated histrionics--the guilty party on the witness stand overcome with remorse, the relatives circling the dying old man's estate. Cry in public and out yourself to be false. Tears were to be private, if shed at all, and then only under the most trying of circumstances.

The death of one's husband made the cut, much less feeling the responsibility for such. But she hadn't been able to cry until she had to face Angel. She'd been stony-faced at the funeral home and determined with the preacher. No service beyond graveside simplicity and that she'd agreed to only for Melba and Ty's sakes. She hadn't been drinking, the blood alcohol tests proved that, and it became a non-issue with the police and the insurance company. One dead deer told the story far better than she could have.

She'd hardened herself into flint, and once the plans to bury Eric were secure, she'd stayed by her friend's side, even as Angel's mother and sisters had drifted in and out, their continual chorus of "our poor girl" tightening Paulina's jaw and wrenching her gut. The boys were there too, but they were scared. Fear she understood. She had managed to shoo them away to Travis and Jason's Dallas apartment on Sunday night. Marcus and Iona had put in separate, brief appearances before leaving for Angel's home and Mark's business and wreaking havoc there. Perhaps Angel would be better served if Paulina were to go there and defend the O'Shea home place and source of income, but she couldn't tear herself from her friend's side.

She'd hardened herself into flint, but the first touch of Angel's tears had twisted her to ashes. She laid her head down and cried as if there were no tomorrow and considered that for her, that was the reality. What tomorrow could there be when love was dead and she was responsible.

Ty's arm went around her shoulders and his face pressed to hers. She felt his tears course down her cheeks and an unfamiliar kiss bestowed. She had been so preoccupied with the business of Eric's death and the possibility that, despite the doctors' assurances, Angel might never wake up, that she had given short shrift to her own son. Had he not cried for the loss of his father? Had he kept a stiff upper lip for William who was disconcerted enough with Mark's death, much less the possibility that his mother might not recover?

If she wasn't the world's worst mother, she could certainly see the position from here.

Jason's tears were interrupted by his laughter, a deep, familiar chortle that broke Paulina's reverie and jerked her head up to look for his father. "Mom, I'm just so happy you're awake!" Man that he was Paulina knew he wasn't ready to be in charge of the O'Shea household--or deal with his relatives who would happily take that role. He squeezed Angel's hand and pressed a kiss onto the back of it, an intimate gesture speaking of a close relationship she had never thought to know with Ty. Was it too late?

***

Angel slipped her hand from Jason's and brushed the dark hair off his forehead with her fingertips. "So I'm really messed up?" The effort of a brief smile brought a wince, and she was able to isolate one more fact: it wasn't just her head. Her face hurt as well.

He shrugged. "What do I know? I'm just a med student."

Even with tear-glazed eyes, she hoped the look she shot him was an adequate warning that he couldn't get away with that.

"Okay. It's not wonderful. You have multiple broken ribs, your right arm was bent behind you somehow and the muscles pulled, your left ankle was smashed, you have one really big bump on your forehead, you've been unconscious for over two days, you no longer have a spleen--but you can live without that--and you look like a raccoon."

"It's a good thing I didn't raise you to spare my feelings."

"That's my mom," he whispered. "But the easy part's behind you, when you were unconscious."

Travis pulled a chair to the side of the bed near her head and laid his head on her pillow. "I keep telling him that with those people skills he should be a proctologist. Don't you think so, Mom?"

She chose to ignore him, although she had not had such attention from her older two since they were eight and ten and put up a relentless campaign to go to Florida and visit every theme park. It hadn't worked because the business was at a crucial stage, and so they'd had to settle for free tickets from a toilet-wholesaler to a professional baseball game. They'd made a weekend of it, visiting the zoo, staying in a suite hotel, near drowning each other at the water park. And she'd come home pregnant with William. They really should have gotten one large hotel room rather than splurging on a suite. She'd cried and cried over the fact of the third child. Now he sat at her feet and clenched the blanket in his oversize hands, his face a study in anxiety and relief. And the very fact of his existence was why she had Paulina beside her here, sharing the strength and dividing the misery.

She was glad it was Paulina she'd awakened to and not her father. She would have reverted to little girl status and it would have taken weeks to recover her place as head of her own household. As inept as Henry Buttons had often proven himself with his all-female family, she would have taken one look at him and he would become 'Daddy' all over again. With her mother or her sisters, she could be made of sterner stuff. They would milk this circumstance for all it was dramatically worth, as if it had happened to them. She did still have to face them, but now she could do so from a position of as much power as she could muster while flat on her back. Her immediate tears were behind her, her shock-tears. She could gain control with just Paulina here and the boys. She could concentrate on the immediate future, the one that had her planning a funeral.

She didn't want to think about it.

"Enough on Jason's special gifts." They all had special gifts. She'd harped on that since they were little. *Don't compare yourselves. Set the standards.* "Let's talk about my ankle." Specifically, the fact that she couldn't feel it.

"Well," Jason shrugged, "it's broken, but they sorted it out and set it and it's in a cast. Wheelchair, crutches, rehab. Outpatient if you behave yourself. You can dance on New Year's Eve."

There wasn't any point in telling him she wouldn't be dancing on New Year's Eve, or maybe ever again. Blood flooded his face with the realization that he'd said the wrong thing, that to mention dancing with her life's dance partner gone... no matter how reluctant he was.

"A proctologist would require too many people skills. How about a radiologist?" Travis hissed.

"Boys..." Angel began, "that's enough. I will walk again, that's what's important."

"Yeah, Mom, you're right. You'll walk again. That's the important thing."

She'd probably limp and have arthritis, and know it was going to rain before the weatherman did, but she would walk again. "You're awfully quiet, William." She turned her attention to him.

"I just want you to come home, Mom. When can you come home?"

"Oh, William." Her heart seized up, her throat tightened at his words, at the anguish on his face. What could she say when she had so little control over this situation? "I just want to come home, too."

Chapter 12

Tuesday morning

They wouldn't let her go home, 'they' being the doctors, the powers-that-were in the hospital, the good solid common sense (or so they told her) of her mother and sisters and even Sarah Neely, that traitor. She had to get stronger, to regain full use of her foot, to consider rehab.

Angel had balked. She'd insisted the funeral director and the preacher and Jason and Travis all meet beside her hospital bed. Her sons were stony-faced with clenched jaws, Mark made over when faced with a job he found distasteful, whether it be firing an employee or counting to ten before launching into a vindictive on a wholesaler's shoddy merchandise. Jason and Travis did not want to be there, but had no choice. William, despite mounting a feeble protest, had left with Paulina and Ty and no backward glances. If she had thought the boys any match for their grandfather, Marcus, she would have excused them from this conversation and made them go to the store, but she knew they weren't. They had fled O'Shea Plumbing Supplies as quickly as their college scholarships could carry them. For Marcus, who thankfully was not here, she would have to have a bigger hammer than either son possessed. In fact, she might have to do the job herself.

But Mark's funeral had to be planned and she would be a part of it. Eric's service would be Wednesday morning, graveside, private, as non-religious as Paulina could get by with. It would be nonexistent if Melba hadn't stuck out her chin and shed tears. At least that was the story according to Sarah. Angel looked cautiously around her hospital room. Was Sarah hidden in a corner, ready to relay this most private of conversations to the world? The men mistook her caution for paranoia and she was treated with kid gloves. As she should be.

Rather than split the grieving over two days, she agreed to the already tentative date of Wednesday afternoon for Mark's service, even though she wouldn't be out of the hospital.

"I'm sorry, Mom," Jason said. "I'll come stay with you." He and Travis sat one on either side of her bed. Reverend Jones and the funeral home director were gone.

"No. You have to be there. Mother can come stay with me."

Her sons cocked eyebrows in unison.

"Well, she can. I'll tell her it's her duty."

"Rather than holding court with Iona?"

"Jason, you have become much too cynical."

"Three years of med school will do that to you."

"Then you will need to find your humanity in residency."

He scowled. "Maybe they'll let you out for the service and then put you back in."

"Like I'm a doll on a shelf."

"Mom…"

"I'll ask. It's tomorrow. I may be lifting weights by then." She paused. "Mother and Iona? It's..." she let her voice trail off, afraid of what she might ask. Were the two staking claims to *her* house, running roughshod over *her* sons, making nuisances of themselves with *her* friends?

Her sons exchanged looks, a shrugged shoulder, a grimace, an unspoken language these two had perfected over their lifetimes. She had thought only twins did this, but Jason and Travis had managed to be just as close, although separated by two years. Now, without a word, they debated what to tell her. The truth would do nicely, but she waited to see what they would come up with.

"Grandmother Delores has been down here a lot." Jason's opening volley was a cautious shot across the bow. "That's left Grandma Iona with the house and the food from the church ladies."

Not bad. Iona would be a stranger to most of them. She would be on her grieving best behavior, ready to keen at the slightest mention of her son's name. Which, considering they hadn't seen Iona for more than an accumulated two days in the last five years, would be a good thing.

Travis picked up the story. "Uncle Marshall got in Sunday. He went to the store yesterday to help Grandpa Marcus who was down there all Saturday, but he didn't stay long. I think it was too much for him, seeing Yancey pull his hair out and wanting to pull Grandpa's. He said it was his way of coping with Dad's death, to work."

Oh, her head hurt. "Yancey or Marcus?"

"Both, probably, but Grandpa said that. I don't think Yancey's particularly happy with him there."

Understatement. A kitchen-war at her home, her

business under siege from an incompetent old boozer who had never appreciated what his son had built... Rehab was looking pretty damn good.

"I guess I need to speak to Yancey."

"I think you need to call off Grandpa."

"I can't do that from here." She looked from one to the other. "You two need to get back to work and school."

"Mom..."

She held up her hand to Jason's protest. "Thursday. You need to get back Thursday. In the meantime, you go home and relieve Yancey at the store although I know you don't either one want to do it and send him down here. Tell him to put his gas on the company card."

"Mom..."

"I'll talk to him and we'll figure out what to do about Marcus."

"Mom, he won't ruin the business before you get back."

"Don't underestimate your grandfather. Trust me when I say that Yancey will not argue with you when you suggest he leave."

Again, they exchanged looks. "Yeah, but who's going to rescue us?"

"You just get between your grandfather and the phone and the customers. Don't let him sign a thing, not even a receipt for merchandise. Preferably, make him go home to whatever current wife he has."

"That's the bump on your head talking. He's not going anywhere."

"Then I'd best have a speedy recovery before there's nothing left to come home to."

Wednesday morning

Paulina had long been accused of having a steel rod where her spine should be. That it began in her ass and worked its way to her brain was usually left understood, but unspoken. This morning, sitting beside Eric's casket, the sun doing its unrelenting best to make everyone miserable, even those under the funeral home tent, this morning, she was thankful for the steel. All she needed was a stiff upper lip to complete her physical ensemble.

Her linen suit itched and pulled in places unknown before. She was sweating down her back, her hair limp on her neck, her thighs screaming to get out of the hose she had foolishly worn. It was June, for Chrissake! Where was her mind? In professional mode, that having pushed aside grieving-widow mode. She didn't want to be a professional, she didn't want to be a grieving widow, she wanted to be…

… anywhere else. *Anywhere.* Sitting for the bar exam when she was twenty-five, even in the prolonged and wretched labor which gave her Ty when she was thirty. Waking up in the ditch when she was fourteen…

Good god, she was desperate, if that were a better alternative. She stole a surreptitious glance around, trying to keep her breathing normal. Everywhere there were people: the sympathetic, the truly mournful, the idly curious. The O'Shea boys were there and that made her doubly sad. How could they stand it? Then, to do it all over this afternoon? She had to be strong, she had to be strong, she had to be strong.

Yes, being fourteen again was a preferred alternative.

Ty's hands clutched his knees and his left leg began the tremor-dance Eric's did when he was nervous.

Funny, she had known that, that Ty was like his father in that respect, but it had never done an irritating dance up her spine before. He had to quit. Borrowing a bit of steel from her pseudo-backbone, she calmly placed her hand atop his, interlacing their fingers. He turned his hand over and squeezed hers.

The boy had a grip. She winced, then looked over at him, at Eric's eyes and tear-tipped lashes. She smiled weakly. *We're in this together*, she wanted to say, hoped the look conveyed all. His knee stilled and he nodded.

Her stomach clenched and her heart seemed to stop, then start reluctantly, each beat pushing the next. Yes, to be fourteen again and not here, to be innocent of so much and yet guilty as sin.

Preferable.

***

Fourteen had not been a good year for Paulina. Not that many of them had up to that point and certainly not any that followed for a while. The family's finances were always on shaky ground, Brady Powers having chased every get-rich-quick scheme to come through Texas. Betty, his ever-present enabler, assured him when things didn't work out that it wasn't his fault. In retrospect, Paulina found it to be an odd juxtaposition of characters: her courtroom experience told her that Betty should be abrader, not abettor. Her steady job as bookkeeper at a mortgage company and Brady's ability to find just enough work to support his next scheme were all that stood between the family and bankruptcy.

But Betty was no fool. She knew what she had in her only child by the time Paulina was six. Bright and bright-eyed, if not a particularly pretty child, Paulina's talents were polished to within a fare-thee-well. Betty took her to museums and zoos on free admittance days, bartered her gardener's green thumb for piano lessons. As an adult, it would strike Paulina as fitting, and not a little ironic, that she had, for good or ill, depended on flowers for much of her sustenance and support, be it from her mother or her husband. But if she was her mother's hot-house plant, she was her husband's wildflower.

By twelve, Paulina had her mother's schemes figured out. The woman saw her as yet another entrée into the world of financial security. College and scholarship were words never far from Betty's vocabulary and if the mother saw them as financial gain, Paulina saw them as her only sure escape.

She was never popular; quick-thinking, outspoken young women have to find their niche in society, and junior high and high school are seldom the providers. Noting this, Betty was determined to move Paulina's social position to a higher rung and for her fourteenth birthday--and over Paulina's very strong objections--she planned a slumber party.

Over the course of the night, the six girls, three in their upper social strata who had dared each other to come and two who could legitimately be called of Paulina's social rank, grew bored with the music and the dancing and the discount store make-up Betty had lavishly provided. When two of her social superiors (and Paulina had always known her social rung) came back from the bathroom with a bottle of Brady's Scotch they'd pinched from the den, Paulina was tempted to awaken her mother. But she figured whatever nonsense they got up to served Betty right. She hadn't meant to drink, but it wasn't any fun watching everyone else and before she could blink, she had lifted Brady's car keys from the hook by the kitchen door, the member of the party with driving experience was leading the way, and the six of them were huddled in the old sedan to drive once around the block.

It hadn't happened that way, of course. Five blocks from the house, the street petered out into a country road. Turning the vehicle around became an issue as the road narrowed. They argued and the driver, taking another swig of the Scotch someone else had brought along, thrust the car into Reverse and pushed down hard on the accelerator. They were doing fine, shrilly screaming as they crowded to see out the back window and shouting "oh, I think I'm gonna die!" at the top of their lungs, until the first curve. The road went to the right and they continued straight into the oak trees.

Paulina awakened in the ditch. On her back, her robe covered in mud, the one member of the party she might have once considered a friend, atop her. That they had all survived was due to luck and the alcohol-infused relaxed state of their bodies. The stiff steel car had not fared so well.

There was enough finger pointing to go around and Brady and Betty barely escaped a lawsuit. They didn't have anything to take, they told the lawyer, the house was rented, the one car which was paid for was wrecked, and there was no money in the bank. Eventually, calmer heads prevailed and a no-harm-done attitude won the day.

But harm had been done. Paulina became an outcast, cementing the hard shell she would later use to good advantage in her worlds of law and business. She vowed never to follow someone else's ill-conceived plan again. That of course did not make her a leader; it made her alone. And it hurt deeply to be so. But, chin high as she studied herself in the bathroom mirror, at the age of fourteen and one month, bearing the mental scars of four weeks of ostracism, she swore not to drink again. She never had.

However, rising from the funeral home chair, steadying herself on Ty's arm, looking for the last time upon Eric's coffin, her legs threatened to buckle at the knees. At that point, she would have gladly abandoned her lifetime pledge and drank herself into a stupor all over again.

***

Waiting was not Angel's strong suit. One would have thought it might be, given the ballgames, the Scout meetings, the late nights, she had waited through. Lying in the hospital bed, the noises of the hallway whispering under the door, the shush of the machines still annoyingly attached to her, she felt herself on pins and needles. It went beyond the drugs she knew still rushed about inside her. If she could have jumped out of her skin--hell, slunk out of it--she would have. Anything not to be here.

Not that the dual funerals were high on her list of places to be either. No, she wanted to be in Cancun, which is where the four of them were supposed to be. She glanced at the date written on the erase-board under the mounted TV. Yes, in one week, they were supposed to be on the beach, already having killed off the first--or second--round of margaritas and guacamole and pico.

145

Her toes were supposed to be digging in the sand, not invisible beneath a sheet and a brace. She was supposed to be falling out of the top of her swimsuit, not baring all to the world every time someone wandered in to check on her injuries.

Waiting was hell.

Sarah Neely had offered to stay with her. God bless Sarah. She hadn't wanted her company--or anyone else's for that matter--which is why she had turned down her mother's reluctant offer in spite of previously threatening the boys with it. Delores wanted to be at the funerals, to see and be seen. To grieve. To hold the hands of the grandsons who, Angel was sure, wouldn't let her. The boys would stand shoulder to shoulder, heads bowed...

Angel shuddered. She couldn't continue down that path.

She looked at the clock. Six. Shouldn't someone be back here? Anyone?

Waiting. Hurry up and wait. Her mantra.

She twisted to look out the window, felt her head slide against her dirty hair. That would make her feel better, getting a clean head. Surely there was something for patients in her condition, something put on the hair to clean it. She'd ask. The last time her hair had felt this way was Cancun.

Their first summer there. For people who knew each other so well, there were still things to find out. Mark and Eric and Paulina had gone deep-sea fishing. She had awakened with a sour stomach--margarita-toxicity was Mark's diagnosis--and knew that a day in a tossing boat would not aid the situation. She had bowed out, taken her refund-chit which the resort graciously offered, and when she felt better that afternoon, gone to the spa and cashed it. A massage was followed by hair-braiding.

She still couldn't believe she had done it. The girl in the salon took her shoulder-length hair and finely braided shells and beads into it from her face to the crown. She looked different; she felt exotic. So she took herself to the boutique at the resort three doors down and bought a flowing caftan in a red hibiscus print. She positioned herself in the lobby where they couldn't miss her and waited for them to arrive from the boat.

An hour passed and her patience started growing thin. As she had just sworn off alcohol for the evening--or at least the next hour or two--she was sipping bottled water and planning the menu for their annual Fourth of July pool party when she heard Mark's voice followed by Eric's laughter and a tone from Paulina that could only be described as sarcastic. Angel rearranged her caftan, patted her hair, sat up straight and shot them a smile.

They walked right past her. Not even a glance. Past the front desk, out to the cabana area, she watched them go. "Didn't Angel say she'd meet us here?" Mark stopped at the patio's edge and peered toward the pool. He put his fists on his hips and did a slow circle, taking in the lobby. He went past her once again.

She did not look that different. Did not.

"Maybe she's still sick," Paulina explained and won a point in Angel's book.

"Or," Eric said as he mimicked Mark's moves, "maybe she's hidden in plain sight." His eyes had roved past her, then riveted back. He quirked a smile and she rose with a sweep of her flowery skirt and walked towards them. Eric was punching Mark in the arm. Still, she had to be standing in front of him to get him to see her.

Paulina, in the meantime, was speechless. Her mouth dropped open, then closed. She reached to touch Angel's beaded hair, withdrew her hand. "I'll be damned," she said softly.

"What got into you?" Mark demanded. "Are you going home like that?"

She hadn't thought that far, just that this would be fun. But she cocked her hip and crossed her arms under her breasts.

"Yes," she said, and she did. She wasn't the only middle-aged woman on the plane so adorned, and Mark made sure to point out every "crazy old girl" at the terminal gate. Not that doing something because everyone else was doing it gave any weight to spurious behavior in the O'Shea family, but there was safety in numbers and he couldn't upbraid someone else's wife.

She'd have worn those beads for a year if her head could have stood it. As it was, she gave them up right after making her point, that she was not invisible--and she could do what she wanted.

Except for today. Today she was invisible and she couldn't do what she wanted. In a bitter moment, Angel realized it would be a long time before she could again.

Chapter 13

Four days later

"So this is rehab?"

"No, this is re-hell. I've finished with hell one and now I'm having to do it all over just in a different location. Therefore, re-hell."

"For how long?"

"A couple of days. They promised. Occupational therapy so I can go beat up on Marcus. Give him something else to occupy himself."

Paulina rolled her eyes.

Angel sighed. "Just till I learn some exercises and my ribs mend enough I won't injure myself breathing."

"That's a better answer." Paulina turned from the mini-blinds in the large window and balanced herself on the wide sill. Someone shorter would have leaned their elbows; she could almost sit. Angel lay in the bed. She was nearly wire-free, only a heart monitor in evidence and that not hooked up. The threat of it remained and Paulina felt that might have been all that kept her friend on her back and not struggling to get up and lurch down the hall to freedom.

Tough week. Tough, uncompromising week. The funerals, the relatives. Getting rid of everyone had seemed to be an easy task until she had undertaken it. She'd had to resort to rudeness to evict Melba Eubanks. And Paulina's rudeness would get most people brought up on charges for verbal assault. Angel's house was still an encampment. Paulina knew because William had moved over with them.

"Is my home still standing?" Angel asked.

So she had an inkling of what was transpiring. Good. Paulina didn't have to mince words. "Yes."

"And William has moved to your place?"

"Lock, stock, and video game player." She studied her sandal-clad toes. "I believe Jason and Travis did a reconnaissance and removed--let's see, how did they put it?-- items of value from your house to ours."

Angel nodded. "They told me. The hunting guns. My silver." She shut her eyes and rested her head against the pillow. "What must you think of our families if my sons don't trust them not to pawn the goods?"

Paulina chuckled. "I'd like to think you would have offered similar protection had our roles been reversed."

Angel cracked an eye and Paulina hung her head in shame and guilt. "Or maybe it wouldn't have happened had you been driving."

"I'd been drinking."

"I was going too fast." God, she hated admitted that, had spent the last ten days trying to justify that night, trying to get the courage pulled together for this discussion with Angel. Trying to avoid this discussion with Angel.

"Not then. No, you weren't speeding then."

"Ang, don't--"

"No, Paulina, I was sitting behind you. I could see the speedometer. You weren't speeding."

Paulina took a sharp breath, narrowed her eyes. "You watch my speed when I'm driving?"

"Not usually..." Angel's voice trailed off and she blushed. "Okay, sometimes."

Paulina clutched at the window sill until her knuckles whitened. There would never come a time when she wasn't judged, would there? It wasn't bad enough to have convicted herself. No, she was watched by her friend.

A memory flew through her thoughts, niggled her conscience. Watching Paulina had probably been a good thing for Angel to do. Would ironies never cease?

So she sought the words she hadn't been able to say. "Angel, I am so sorry."

"Pauli, it wasn't your fault."

Quit being angelic! She wanted to scream it. Instead, "Oh, but it was, it has to be. Someone has to be at fault."

"That's the prosecutor talking. Get back on the side of the defense."

Now she really felt bad, if that were possible. She knew there was a place worse than worst and she was there. Feeling bad, worse, worst had been her yoke since waking in the emergency room, but she had never been given to confession.

And now, when each was all the other had left, was not the time to start. Still...

"Do you not wonder what would have happened had someone else been driving?"

"Someone would have a DUI."

"All alcoholic content being the same as mine."

Angel rubbed at her legs with her good hand,

wouldn't raise her eyes to Paulina's. Finally, just when Paulina thought she would have to say something, she spoke. "I would have been too pokey from the get-go. I don't drive the speed limit anyhow as my children have reminded me often enough. The deer would have been gone before we got there." She lifted a shoulder as if to shrug. "Eric would have done the same as you." She looked at Paulina and a tear trickled down her cheek. "Mark would have been at hyper-speed before we left the club. We'd have been down the road before the deer crossed." She quirked a little smile and sniffled. "Paulina, don't try and second guess the circumstances. They happened. I don't like this world I've been brought to. I want to go home in more ways than one." Now the tears were flowing and Paulina stood there helplessly, unsure what to do. What had she wrought with her game of what if? "I want my husband."

"I want mine," Paulina answered. Slowly she walked to the bed and sat down gingerly on its edge.

"I feel so helpless. I am so helpless."

"You have me."

"Oh!" A cry caught in Angel's throat and Paulina found an even lower rung of guilt than she knew existed. As Angel cried against her shoulder, her own tears started.

They sat there, clinging to each other for a while. Noises from the rehab floor filtered in. Somewhere a phone rang. The sun shifted its position just enough that the room cast into shadow.

"You know, Paulina, I was thinking." Angel pushed away from her. Her eyes were red and her skin splotchy. She blinked back more tears. "I've had a lot of time to think." She wiped at her eyes and pushed on the bed to straighten herself. "It's better this way. Not necessarily that you and I survived, but that one of us from each family did. What would it have been for Ty to have lost you both, or William both of us? This way, we can carry on somehow. We can keep our families going. Different, sure, but going."

Paulina's stomach knotted. "You are truly too good, you know?"

Angel shook her head. "I'm just selfish. It would have been better for the business if Mark had lived, but..." she bit at her lip, "but he didn't. So it's me. And as soon as I can, I'll be there. And, William and I will be okay. Just like you and Ty will."

"If that's your idea of selfish, we should all be such."

"We'll be okay, you'll see."

"I've no doubt." And she didn't. It wasn't the destination Paulina was concerned with, it was the road there.

Fate's Third Decision

Mark and Eric

Prologue
Standifer

It had taken Les Standifer two years, four months, and six days, to forgive Paulina Eubanks.

Having spent a good portion of his adult life rotating between AA meetings and the drunk tank, he considered himself lucky if he woke up in his own bed and not in the alley behind his current, favorite bar. Not that he'd remember how he got either place. Two women had thrown up their hands in disgust with him, and he counted himself fortunate he'd never fathered children.

So a smart-ass, tight-skirted, big-breasted district attorney really held no threat for him. He'd been there, done that since before she was born. Didn't it figure: the one time--the *one* fucking time--he'd let himself get behind the wheel drunk, he was caught. And that was just because his buddy was drunker. So there, in court, with Missy Assistant DA--if she was really any good why was she just the assistant?--staring holes in him, he'd made up his mind. No more. He'd not have her kind of woman looking down her nose at him again. Not ever.

Resolve may have got him sober, but stubbornness kept him there. He'd stayed sober for over two years before their paths crossed again. The same buddy drinking and disturbing the peace got a sober Standifer arrested while trying to calm him down. Perhaps, ADA

Eubanks suggested, he should try a new set of friends?

He didn't know then that she was on the verge of giving up the law, going into financial planning, trying a set of new friends for herself. The law had lost its appeal for her, just as his buddy lost his and landed in jail for six months.

Being laid off at the cable company that same day had tempted him to his old ways. That's what had happened the day he and the buddy were arrested. So, he'd asked her sarcastically, with as much disdain as he could muster, did she know of a job for a retired drunk?

Could he tend bar?

Surely, surely she was kidding.

Who better to know when someone else had had enough, she stated.

Who better indeed.

He'd applied for the job and she'd vouched for him. For the first time in longer than he could remember, he didn't want to disappoint someone.

He found out she didn't drink, not even celebratory sips of champagne. She wouldn't tell him why. If her husband knew, and Standifer didn't think he did, he wouldn't tell either. The woman was a mystery, and he respected her for it.

But standing at the police barricades at two in the morning, staring down the narrow road to the bridge beyond, hearing the thump of the retreating helicopter, Standifer was incredulous. It couldn't be the O'Sheas and the Eubanks. They were just at his bar. The birthday boy was potted, to be sure, but he'd seen the key be handed over to Paulina and she wouldn't have handed it back.

"Mr. Neely," he called over the barricade. He clutched the top of it, leaned toward the Neely car.

155

Others were parked around him, the highway patrol trying to get the onlookers, who seemed to have materialized out of nowhere, to move on. Now that there was nothing else to see, most of them were. Standifer couldn't go.

Adam Neely raised his head at the sound of Standifer's voice, gazed toward him, through him. Suddenly, the insurance man looked his age. Gone was the easy smile Standifer had seen when he'd bid him goodnight. Neely, always kind, always polite, had ever had a joke for the bartender. He liked the man, although society would no more put him in his company than that of the people on the gurneys.

Adam waved him past the barricade. Standifer hesitated, looked at the young officer striding toward him. Neely said something to him, and he nodded and Standifer raced around to the car. He knelt by Adam. Behind the man, his wife sat staring through the windshield, tears rolling down her cheeks.

"People were saying..." Standifer started and Adam closed his eyes and nodded. "Are they... are they all okay?"

Neely slowly shook his head. He raised two fingers, as if speech were beyond him.

"Which?" Fifteen years ago he'd have wished to see Paulina Eubanks zippered up in a black bag, but not now. Not any of them.

"They, ah, they careflighted Eric and Mark." Neely's voice was a croaky whisper and he pinched the bridge of his nose with his fingers, stretching his fingers onto his forehead and rubbing it. "I'm sorry, Standifer, I..."

He ignored Neely's hesitation, plunged on in his quest for answers. The highway patrol might not be able to tell him what he wanted to know, but Adam Neely could. And would. "What about Angel?" He drew a shaky breath. "Paulina?" Normally he would have addressed them as the club demanded, Mrs. O'Shea, Mrs. Eubanks. Somehow, that no longer seemed important. Their husbands had been careflighted. They had been…

Loud voices, then a shout or two came from the other side of the drop toward the river. Standifer stood, gripped the top edge of the driver's door and stared. Neely turned toward the noise, hoisting his left leg into the car. He stared through the windshield. Two sets of men appeared, each bearing a gurney. They released the metal legs, let them roll toward the awaiting ambulance. Each bore a zippered body bag and Standifer had his answer.

Chapter 14

Monday afternoon after the accident

"**E**ric..." The voice on the other end of the line stalled, faded. Eric reached behind himself for the kitchen chair and sat down heavily. He dropped the cane and it clattered noisily on the terrazzo. He expected his mother to come running to his rescue, to check on him as she had been doing repeatedly for the last forty-eight hours, but there were no footsteps, no "Eric, are you okay?"s to haunt him. Perhaps she'd collapsed in exhaustion and God knew she should. Protecting him, protecting Ty, protecting Paulina's things from her scavenging family... Melba Eubanks was due the Medal of Honor in Defense of her Family. Try as he might, he couldn't see Betty Powers defending his home place in his absence. Melba was no saint, but she had at least been-there, done-that with the loss of a spouse. He turned his attention back to the phone, to Mark's voice as it found its volume and started over.

"Eric, shit, I'm sorry, I can't seem to put two words together to make any sense."

"It's okay, Mark. I feel the same way." When there was silence again, he added, "They let you out?"

"With three pages of instructions, five appointment cards and into Jason's care. There may be some use to having a doctor in the family after all." It sounded rehearsed, as if Mark had been saying it as they wheeled him out of the hospital, and then repeated as often as he could, a neutral subject, just as Eric was only too happy to talk of anything and anyone but Paulina.

"I'll see what I can do with Ty."

"Have you... have you..." Mark cleared his throat as it closed up and his words turned to gravel, then rushed what he was trying to say, "Have you made Paulina's arrangements?"

"Yesterday." Ellen on one side of him, Melba on the other, Ty enraged that he hadn't been included in the trip to the funeral home. Yes, he'd made those arrangements and determined that as soon as he spiritually could, he'd go back and make his own. He would spare Ty what he and Paulina had not thought to spare each other.

"Good. Then come over here and help me."

"Ohhh." The groan was involuntary. It slipped from his throat before he could stop it. How could Mark ask this of him?

He continued as if he'd heard nothing. "I'm sorry to ask, but the boys are spinning their wheels and Henry and Delores are beside themselves and Iona is more useless than teats on a boar hog. And I think I'll kill my father if he opens his mouth one more time and..."

Eric stopped him. "I'll come as soon as I round up a ride."

"Trav should be in your driveway."

Eric pushed himself to a shaky stand. Wheeling in was Angel's SUV. Eric's heart stopped, then started again, when he saw it was Travis driving, William riding shotgun. The boy bolted out of the front seat before it even stopped. Eric clicked off the phone and sat back down in order to pick up the cane. Ty materialized and grabbed it, helped him to stand again, offered his dad his arm. William didn't bother ringing the doorbell but was on Eric's other side, his breath fast.

Eric must have been the last one notified that he was going to the O'Shea's.

"We need to tell your grandmother."

"I told Aunt Ellen. Gran's taking a nap."

That explained that.

"How's your dad doing, William?" He asked the question cautiously as they eased down the wide front steps and into the circular drive. Travis had positioned the vehicle as close to the front steps as possible. And as much as he hated to admit it, he could slip into the seat through the sliding door much more easily than had it been a car. But still… it was Angel's.

"How's he doing? He's not." William watched as Ty dove in first, waited to catch Eric if he fell getting in while William stood guard outside. As he slammed the door, the child with Angel's eyes looked at Eric and tightened his mouth into a straight line. "None of us are."

***

So okay, Mark had to admit, it was a chicken shit thing to do. So sue him.

He wanted to be upstairs, in his chair beside his bed, his legs raised, his remote control, the one he knew where all the buttons were on it, in his right hand, something alcoholic in his left. He wanted to see Angel coming out of the bathroom, her summer gown swishing about her calves, her bare feet sporting the latest color-of-the-month polish, her face free of make-up, her hair combed for the night. He wanted to hear her sigh as she got into bed, plump her pillow with a great deal of fuss, and finally ask him how long he thought it would be before he would shut that damn sports show off and get in bed. He wanted to stroke her cheek, feel the velvety smoothness of her breast, taste…

He wanted to be anywhere but in his den, imprisoned downstairs by his sons until night came because getting him up the stairs was going to be a Monumental Effort and he, Mark, had Things To Do. Things best accomplished, to their group thinking, in the den. Delores and Henry had taken over the downstairs guest room, and even if he'd had the heart to use it, he hadn't the heart to kick them out of it. Anyway, he wanted to be in his own bed come night. But making him stay down smacked of reverse tough-love. He knew it for what it was: fear and gratitude. The boys had been afraid he too would die and now that it looked like he might actually make it, broken bones and bruised body aside, they were so grateful they put all the burdens of leadership back on his shoulders. Did they not know who had really run the family all these years? Were his sons as blind as he had been?

So, no, it wasn't fair of him to call Eric, to make him live through this all again. But he couldn't think and he wouldn't be bullied by the funeral home director, a man he had little respect for, an opinion, Mark had to admit, based mostly on the man's inability to do anything mechanical with his hands. The old bastard probably figured he was finally going to get back some of the money he'd paid O'Shea Plumbing all these years.

He had to whip his attitude into shape before they

showed up. The appointment was at four. He'd have been better off to go to the funeral home, but he physically couldn't make it. The director could make a house call, and here's where Rev. Johns had finally come in handy. The preacher was due at 3:30 and he was about to earn the O'Shea tithe.

The front door creaked open and an unfamiliar thump-slide echoed down the hall. Mark nodded to its rhythm, mentally denoting the change in echo when Eric crossed the hall runner. The boys should have picked that up. Now there were more footsteps, slow and measured, one, no two, sons following Eric. Hovering, no doubt. Making the man too nervous to move. It would be a miracle if he made it to the den without falling.

"Aren't we a fine pair?" Eric stood in the wide archway, leaning heavily on the cane, one hand atop the other. He waited for Ty to bring the hard-seated dining table chair and place it close to Mark.

Mark's eyes swept up and down his friend's frame. "You look like shit."

Eric snorted. "And they'll never get you out of that lounger. What possessed you to get in it?"

"Hell, he insisted." Travis tossed the car keys in the basket on the mantel, Angel's spot for them since Jason, as a toddler, had plucked her keys from the kitchen table and lost them behind the crib. Lost them for six months, long after they'd had a new set made. Lost them until it was time to move from the rundown trailer to the disaster that was their first apartment and the crib had been moved. "Don't know how Mother's done it all..." His voice trailed off and he stood there, shaking his head and pinching his lips together. Stood there and looked like he did, Mark thought, at that age, a mirror image to the heartbreak of finding out Angel was pregnant and life had just taken a turn for the different. He'd long ago quit thinking of it as for the worse. This particular set of events was a turn for the worse.

Worst. There could be no set of circumstances worse than this. Had just one of the women died, the remaining couple would have pulled the one left together, stood guard, been an anchor. But this? Good Lord!, this situation left the two least equipped to handle a disaster on their own... on their own. He echoed Travis's question in his mind. "How *had* Angel done it all these years?" How had she handled him and the boys and the house and...

"You got any more Scotch?"

...and Marcus, her father-in-law. How had she even survived around that man?

"You've drank it all, Grandpa."

From the mouths of babes. William had had about all the family he could stand. Mark could read it in the set of his jaw, the glare of his eyes, the way his shoulders hunched as he squatted by the empty fireplace grate and ran his hands through Dweeb's thick fur as the dog lolled between him and Ty.

Marcus stood in the doorway to the kitchen. He stiffened and rattled the ice in his glass. Crystal. Good God, he had Angel's prized crystal from the set she'd pieced together at the online auction site after winning a starter set at a charity sale. Not normally given to caring what he drank his Scotch out of, Mark had finally given in to her pleas--and the temptation of a bottle of 25-year-old single malt she bought for Christmas--and done a taste test blindfolded. The crystal, the old glasses, a plastic cup, something she borrowed from Paulina that was the right size and shape. The crystal made a difference; he'd had to admit it. So he'd bought her service for twelve and they only drank their liquor and wine out of the good stuff.

Now he watched as his father threatened to shake it so hard, it broke. Not at fifty bucks a glass. He tried to twist in his chair, threaten him non-verbally until he had to do otherwise.

"You'd think," the older O'Shea continued, oblivious to the frigid air that had settled in the room, "that with all the do-goodin' goin' on around here this week, someone would have thought to include a few bottles with their chicken casseroles!" He drew a deep breath and wheezed. "Damn chicken mus' be the cheapest meat."

Oh, sweet Jesus. "Trav--"

"Grandpa, let's go get some more." Travis was one step ahead of Mark as he pulled the keys out of their basket. "You can pick it out. You got any money?"

Marcus shot a harsh look from his son to his grandson and pressed his lips together, deciding not to press his luck. "What do you think I am, boy, a mooch? I got money!" He slammed the glass down on the countertop and followed Travis out the front door.

"Well, I think he's a mooch." Mark shifted his weight in the lounger. "William, when they get back you tell your brother I'll cover his losses because there's no way in hell Grandpa is willing to pay for what he wants."

Eric chuckled. "I'll take your mooch and raise you a poacher."

Mark drew back and considered his friend. "Poaching?"

"Mother swears the Powers women are after Paulina's things."

164

Ty snorted. "Like Mom's things will fit anybody." He pulled on Dweeb's head and the dog transferred his attention to him.

"I think Gran has jewelry in mind," Eric amended.

"Yeah, I know." Ty gave the dog's belly a final forceful rub and looked up at the men. "When she figured out what was going on, she had me get Mom's jewelry case and hide it."

Eric closed his eyes and shook his head. "She what? Where is it?"

"I gave it to William."

Mark joined Eric in staring at their sons. "And it is where?"

The boys looked at each other. "I put it in the shell drawer below the gun case. Hid the key back where you keep it."

"Oh, boys." Mark shook his head.

"Can't it stay here?" Ty pleaded. "Dad, they never come around, not even Grandma and Grandpa. I don't even know who some of those people are! Mom didn't like them. Why are they here now? And they don't have any right to go through her things!"

"I know," Eric answered. "I know."

"Can her case stay here? Why…"

"It's fine with me. If it's okay with--"

Mark nodded his head. "William, do we need to send anything home with Ty?"

"The liquor and Mom's crystal." *Everyone* had been involved in the crystal hunt.

"I think we can let that slide. Why don't you guys take Dweeb for a run? Eric and I have business to discuss."

They pushed themselves off the hearth. "C'mon,

boy." William patted his thigh and the dog leaped to his side. "Let's go chase squirrels, what say?" Dweeb barked and they left noisily through the patio doors.

"That was remarkably easy," Eric murmured. "No protest."

"I'm sure they have things to discuss."

"Motherless boys." Eric rested his elbows on his knees and buried his face in his hands.

Mark studied his friend. He wasn't unshaven, but there was gray visible in his beard and Mark had never noticed it before. Lines, not from labor in the sun, etched the sides of his face and his back had an old man's hunch. Had he aged as much in three days as Eric? "Tell me what you did about Paulina's service."

"At the cemetery, Wednesday morning at ten." The words came through his fingers.

"I had thought Wednesday afternoon for Angel." He drew a deep breath. "I can't do them both in one day. I just can't. I'm sorry, Eric."

"I don't expect you to come."

"But I have to."

"You just said..." Eric's voice sharpened and he straightened up. His eyes were hooded, bloodshot. How to age a decade in a day.

Mark reached for the glass of water on the side table, took a deep swallow. There was no way to say this but to *say it*. "Would Paulina turn in her grave if we did them at the same time? Can we expect our family and friends to go through it all twice?"

"What are you talking about?" Of all times for Eric to be obtuse.

"Paulina and Angel. The same people will come to both services. Let's just have one. It won't bother Angel none."

"Hell, Mark," and Mark couldn't tell if laughter or sarcasm was in the back of Eric's voice, "it won't *bother* Paulina. If her cosmos is to be believed, she'll never know."

"And if it's not?" Mark couldn't believe he was on the verge of laughter.

"When I see her, I'll tell her it was all your idea."

***

To put the icing on the cake, so to speak, Ty didn't own a suit.

"Mother, what does it matter?" Eric found himself asking Tuesday morning. "Dress slacks…"

"All he owns are khakis." Melba Eubanks stood in the center of his kitchen and looked accusatorily at her son where he sat at the small table. Ty was staring out the kitchen window as if making a detailed count of the blades of grass. The rest of the household was still abed or already at the pool. He hadn't thought his headaches could be any worse until his mother started this conversation.

"Then he can wear khakis."

She shifted her weight.

"Or you can buy him a suit."

"Dad, I don't want…"

Eric held his hand up for silence. "I don't care." He turned his hand and buried his forehead in it, spoke to the tabletop. "Go with your grandmother to the mall. Let her buy you something suitable." He dared look at them. "I'll pay you back, Mom."

"I can afford to buy him something suitable," she

huffed.

"Fine." Far be it for him to argue. He'd make it up to her at her birthday or Christmas.

"Dad."

"I don't think you have a horse in this race."

"I am the horse in this race."

Eric quirked a smile at his son's chagrin. "Then make sure you resemble the front end until you get back here."

Ty rolled his eyes. "C'mon, Gran, let's get going. And you're going to have to buy me pizza for lunch, too."

"Will you be okay here if we're gone over lunch?"

Eric looked up at her. "You should have thought of that before bringing this whole thing up. There's a house full of people awaiting my beck and call."

"Waiting for me to leave, more like it."

"Let me repeat: You're the one who opened this can of worms."

"We'll be quick." She turned to Ty. "Just let me get my purse."

Son and grandson watched her leave the room. "You can always call William if you need help."

"You don't want to take him with you?"

"I can be humiliated on my own, thank you very much."

Footsteps across the terrazzo hall. "Let's go." Melba brushed at her slacks. "I dare not leave this place for too long."

"We're having pizza, Gran, and I'm not eating it in the car."

"I should say not."

Eric listened as the front door closed on their conversation. Now if Brady and Betty would just stay out of his hair, he might survive these next hours.

He scooted his chair so the back of it was to the wall. He could lean his head back and squeeze his body up to the table and rest himself without the exertion of returning to bed or laying himself wide open to the scrutiny of the den. He would have liked to lie in the sun, let the heat burn away his fatigue and pain and worry, but there would be others to deal with. As it was, if he were silent enough he could hide here for hours, essentially invisible to anyone entering the kitchen for a dish or a bottle of water from the fridge. Hidden in plain sight. The idea appealed to him.

Especially since that wouldn't be the case tomorrow. Adding Angel's service to Paulina's had called for a change of plans. With the funeral director and the minister both present, it should have been simpler than it was. Apparently neither man was comfortable with having their preconceptions challenged, much less changed. He had been determined to keep Paulina's service simple and devoid of organized religion, putting it at the cemetery's remembrance garden and not inside the church. However, he found it more important to share Mark's grief and see that Angel was remembered properly. And truly, he couldn't have done two services, so Paulina was along for the ride. Her wish to be cremated wasn't in writing, but she'd told him often enough. He hadn't had the heart to think about it, but after the service, she would be. She'd not specified to him where her ashes should be taken, but he thought Cancun. They'd laughed there and had good times.

It would be one last dunk in the ocean.

Chapter 15

Wednesday morning

Weren't they a fine lot, Mark mused. Two stubborn men who ought to be in wheelchairs, instead were being escorted, canes and crutches, by aging women and hapless sons. Just as soon as the funeral director had pointed him in one direction down the church's aisle and Eric in the other, they had looked at each other and the same thought had pulled them together. "Hell with that," Eric muttered under his breath and they sat together on the O'Shea side, let the family chips fall where they may.

Because they weren't getting through this without each other.

His sons… bless their hearts, as Angel would have said. William was like a colt suddenly turned loose in the back pasture, running in circles from railing to railing, stopping to paw and snort and whinny. Useless to anyone. Jason and Travis were the epitome of fine sons, grown and responsible young men, but hard as they tried, hard as they all tried, they just didn't understand. They were coming at this from another direction. Their mother was dead. The family anchor was gone. He felt far more kinship with William than Jason and Travis. And just when he thought his circle-running days were long gone, too.

The service started. Reverend Johns enjoined them all to prayer. Maybe he should just keep his head down, staring at the linoleum, tracing its pattern in his mind's eye. Why didn't they lay tiles side to side, rather than turning every other one at ninety degrees? Why not take each set of four and make a pattern? Why not...?

Amen. He heard an amen. He looked up at the cross on the wall behind the altar. *You got some explainin' to do*, he thought. *This isn't fair.*

Fair. Angel's favorite four-letter f-word. Would he spend the rest of his life detailing every little thing back to her? *Oh, God.*

He broke. He hadn't meant to cry. He had determined he wouldn't. He would set a stoic example for his sons. Besides, he should be cried out. But, no, the tears came and his shoulders shook. "Dad," William grasped his left hand and held it and Travis circled his brother's shoulders in order to reach him.

But it would be Eric's reaction he would recall. Eric's white-knuckled grip released his own trembling knee and he grasped Mark's other hand and gripped it tightly. And that's the way they made it through the service, a row of men in grief so deep they couldn't prevail without each other.

Saturday
One week after the accident
"I know what you're up to." Miguel gripped the truck steering wheel with both hands as they rumbled toward the river bridge to the country club. The veins stood out on the backs of his sun-darkened hands and the gold of

his worn wedding ring caught a spark of the afternoon sun. "We don't have any clients out this way."

Eric turned his attention from his right-hand man to the road. A week ago he'd ventured down this road in high spirits at the thought of the joke they'd be playing on Mark the next day. *A week ago... God.* He had to stop that mantra. It was consuming his mind, ruining his life. It had even managed to overtake the echo of his accusation to Paulina that she didn't love him any more. And he never thought he'd forget *that* piece of bad timing.

"Well, good. You have me figured out. In that case, we can give up all pretense and you can make a left where the guard rail is gone. Just pull her to a stop and let me out."

"And then what?" Miguel argued even as he followed Eric's instructions, spewing gravel on the shoulder as he U-turned and put the truck's passenger door toward the relative safety of the grass. He stuck the truck in gear and shut off the engine, then twisted in the driver's seat, one arm stretched on the back of the seat, the other draped on the steering wheel. "You gonna walk down there or you want me to carry you?"

"I hadn't thought of going to the water."

"Bullshit."

Miguel *was* pissed if he was swearing in English. Not that Eric didn't know all the choice Spanish words, but if Miguel wanted to emphasize something, he did it plainly and in English. That was one reason the two men had done so well together, had been able to plan the new business with Yancey and Mark. They understood each other on all the necessary levels.

"All I asked for was a ride. You got something better

172

to do than sit here for five minutes, you just go on and do it."

"And you'll get home?"

"I'll hitchhike. Guarantee someone would pick up a cripple."

Miguel huffed. "Then I'd be on crutches when Stella finds out I left you."

"See, my evil plan worked." Eric gave into the smirk and yanked at the door handle, putting his bruised shoulder into it, then nearly toppling out as it gave way. He caught himself and ignored Miguel's grunt of satisfaction.

"You need me to come pick up your sorry ass when it's sitting on the ground or sliding down the embankment, you just yell real loud. I'm gonna sit here in the air conditioning." With that, he started the diesel again, tipped his baseball cap over his eyes and feigned sleep.

Eric steadied himself with the crutch and slammed the door. He pulled his sunglasses from the top of his head and grabbed the cane from where he'd balanced it against the crew cab's back door. Limping, he made his way from the smell of gas and the knock of the engine. Thank goodness for Stella's implied wrath, or Miguel might well have left him long enough to wander down the highway and make him seriously wonder about how to get home.

But if Ty weren't there, there wouldn't be any point in going back, now would there?

He jerked when he heard the slam of the truck door. Now what? Couldn't Miguel damn well leave well enough alone? More noise, metal scraping on metal. Damned if he'd turn around and see what was happening.

He continued limping to where the guard rail was still of a piece. Maybe he could perch there.

Footsteps on the gravel, Miguel's heavy tread, then the screech of a folding chair being opened and plopped down in front of him. "Here," Miguel snarled, "and I am not going to be responsible for you passing out in this heat. You sit and work out those demons and I'm going down to the club and talk that bartender out of some water. You rushed us out of there before…"

Eric waved a hand at him, a grateful dismissal if he'd been called to explain it. He had rushed them out of the sheds on the new property. He couldn't stand being at work, couldn't stand being at home, thought he had to be here… But he wasn't in a mood to apologize just yet. "That would be good." He eased himself into the chair as Miguel held it steady.

"I'll be back in ten minutes."

"Take your time." He laid the crutch on the ground and overlaid his hands on the head of the cane, fixed his gaze on the trees below and the Jaguar-made hole that went through them.

Miguel's footsteps retreated, came back. "Look, boss, Eric…" he hesitated, "you gonna be okay? I'm not gonna come back and find you gone, am I?"

Would that.

"No. I just need to sit for a few minutes. I just need to be here." He broke eye contact with the trees and stared up at Miguel. "And water would be very good for the ride back to town."

***

Mark shifted his weight and pulled on his right knee.

Maybe there was a spot on the top of his head which didn't hurt, but he'd have been at a loss to find it just now. Angel's van racketed roughly over the metal joints of the bridge, each click on the tires jarring him even further. Whose stupid idea was this adventure?

Oh, yeah. His.

Yancey, anger rolling off him like water, broke the silence they'd traveled in from the store. "Looks like you're going to have company. Now I wonder how he got here." Yancey jerked the van sharply to the left, braking only as the turn was completed and he came upon Eric. "I don't suppose *you* thought to bring a folding chair?"

Mark wanted to ask him why all the anger. Was it being taken away from work on a busy Saturday morning or had there been a family commitment he would have felt guilty sharing with Mark? He wanted to ask why all the anger, but he didn't want to know the answer. He had enough anger for both of them. Yancey was mooching on his emotional territory.

"Maybe I can sit in his lap."

That drew a smile. "Well, I didn't bring my camera so don't go having too much fun. I'd hate to lose a prime social media moment." He turned to his boss and friend, dropped the sarcasm. "You really want me to leave you? You want to find out where Eric's chauffeur is?"

Yes. No.

Will you come back?

The thought haunted Mark. They'd--he'd--done that to Jason once, left him at the side of highway. He was being an absolute ass--even for a kid of thirteen. It was supposed to be a family outing, a last one before William was born. Angel was huge and out of sorts, but had

175

agreed to the thirty-minute road trip to the gourmet ice cream parlor in the next town. Halfway back, and in the early dusk, Jason's carping and complaining had finally taken its toll on his male parent. He'd wanted the biggest sundae, wolfed it down, gone after Travis's, which had been spilled over the vinyl seats in the melee. He then added insult to injury by declaring himself thoroughly disgusted that his mother was pregnant. That had been the last straw and Mark had pulled to the side of the rural highway and ordered him out. The look of terror on his face was matched by Angel's, but Mark didn't care. The boy would respect his mother or he could find a new place to hang his backpack.

He'd gotten out of the car, was too flabbergasted not to, and continued to hurl insults as Mark had pulled away. Angel sat there silently, her hands on her swollen belly. Travis went from shock to glee to the realization that if his dad would leave one son by the side of the road, he'd leave two.

Mark had driven over the rise, turned around and come back. Jason was no where to be seen.

He feared Angel would go into labor right then and there. Her breath caught and her hands spasmed. Then, to his silent relief and Angel's audible sigh, the boy's head popped up from the ditch, followed by a body with hands quickly fastening his fly. Taking a leak on the side of the highway. *Jesus!* At least no one had driven down the road and seen him. Mark pulled the car over, Travis opened the door, and Jason got in silently.

He didn't speak to Mark for two weeks, but by then William had arrived and the two older ones had once again found solidarity in each other.

To this day, they were thicker than thieves.

176

"Well?"

Yancey actually expected an answer. "Yes, I want you to leave me. No, I don't care where Eric's chariot is." He pushed on the door. It was still locked. Yancey hit the release and Mark swiveled himself out. He looked through the door window at Eric who hadn't even turned his head at the intrusion. Did the man just not care who was joining him? They could have murder and mayhem in mind at Saturday noon and Eric seemed not to care.

Well, *he* didn't, did he?

If not for William. Okay, if not for Travis and Jason, too. They still needed their dad. Surely, surely they did. God knew he needed them.

It was a sobering thought. At some point he'd stopped needing his dad. What Marcus did annoyed him, threatened him and his business, and though he didn't need him, on a purely emotional, spiritual level, he had to admit that the sight of the old man swaying in the hospital room doorway had buoyed him. That, of course, had lasted all of ten minutes until the old bastard started blaming him for the accident by buying an damned, expensive car.

Surely his sons still needed *him*.

"I think I can manage for a little bit. I'll call your cell." He staggered to a standing position between the crutches. Yancey inched the car forward to allow him to swing the door closed by aiming at it with the right crutch and he limped over to stand behind Eric.

"Well, I know why I'm here. Why are you?" Eric asked the question as he half-turned to Mark. The sunglasses hid his eyes and Mark could only guess at their expression.

"I thought I'd talk to God."

"Get in line." Eric turned back to stare down the embankment.

"You getting any answers?" Mark limped around to the good part of the guard rail and eyed it cautiously.

"I don't think it'll hold you."

"It sure as hell didn't hold a Jag." Mark couldn't help the bitterness. It had so quickly become his way of life. And it had to go. It wasn't him. It wasn't Angel. It wasn't them.

But then, his 'them' was gone.

Bitterness didn't become him, he could hear Angel telling him that from long ago. Long ago when life was narrowed down to too many children and not enough money. They couldn't be bitter, she'd said. The circumstances were their own fault--unintentional, but their own nonetheless--and they'd just have to work through them.

So they had.

But this unintentional circumstance wasn't his fault. Nor Angel's. Nor Eric's. Maybe Paulina's, but he'd not lay blame on the dead.

"Earth to Mark!"

He jerked his head up at Eric's sharp tone. "What?" He slammed the sharp edge out of his tone. "I'm sorry, Eric. I can't focus. What did you say?"

Eric nodded. "Had you named the Jag yet?"

"Named? Oh, yes." Mark chuckled in his throat and shook his head. "Mac."

"For... macintosh green?" There was no reproach in Eric's voice.

"What is that?"

"Precisely." Leave it to Eric to strive for normalcy. "You name your cars for their colors. Radiantly Red became Radar and Moonglow was Luna Light and... hell, I couldn't keep up with them. We had Eric's fuckin' old truck and Paulina's spiffy new car. You had imagination."

"Angel had imagination."

"Had to to see something in you."

This was more like the old Eric, a bit of a tease and a comic. Talking to God must have helped him. Mark needed to get in line and get to it. Eric needed to leave, something not likely to happen until his chariot came back.

Eric continued. "So if it wasn't macintosh green...."

Damn dog with a bone. "Middle-aged crazy. M A C. Mac."

"Angel."

"Angel."

"Served you right."

"I didn't argue. But I was searching for something to explain it with. Jaguars are not called Mac."

Eric shrugged. "I don't know. Kinda' suited."

Eric the obtuse. So much for the help from God. "Who brought you out here?" Pause. Time for pay-back. "Your mother?" He edged it with sarcasm.

"My mother." He took a deep breath, gave his head a slight shake. "My mother is beside herself that I won't need her. She can't make herself go. Which is what she needs to do. Ty and I have to start to be..." Lowering his head, he ran his left hand through his hair, pausing to grasp the back of his head and then pull it up. It took an effort. "Ty and I have to start to be by ourselves. Which doesn't answer your question. Miguel brought me. He's gone to the club for water."

"Why?"

"I'm thirsty."

"No, why do you have to be by yourselves? You've got the good mother of the lot. You need to cash in. William and I don't have anything to offer but a woman who was so grateful I told her to go I barely saw her feet hit the floor and someone who is as uncomfortable with me as I am with her. I let Delores go home with Henry, told her I'd call if I needed her."

"Which was a lie."

"Which was a lie. Because I need someone. There!" He adjusted his crutches. "I've admitted it."

"Can't believe she left you."

"To her credit, she calls everyday. Wants to speak to William. Doesn't trust me to tell her the truth."

"That's because she's your mother-in-law. No doubt you've lied to her before." Eric gave his voice a falsetto. "Oh, yes, Mrs. Buttons, I'll be a gentleman. Angel is safe with me." He looked over the top of his sunglasses.

"Did anyone ever tell you what a smart ass you are?"

"Your wife." He focused on the tree line. "My wife."

"It's only been a week."

"How come it seems like forever? One moment, it's like she never existed. The next that she's coming home any time."

"We are a sad pair. And I don't just mean unhappy."

"Amen."

"But I'm not ready for a come-to-Jesus meeting. I want to wallow a while longer."

Eric snorted. "Even though you know you're going to have to pick yourself up and dust yourself off and get back on that horse."

Mark was silent. Were they really having this conversation? "We sound like women. Real men don't talk like this."

"I turned in my real man badge years ago."

Did he laugh or cry? Both? "Paul... Paulina...." Hell, that was all he could get out over the chortle and the tears. "That is..." He almost doubled over. He wasn't supposed to laugh like this again. Not so soon. Maybe not ever. If he lost his balance, he'd go right down the embankment.

Eric raised a hand to steady him and clutched at his wrist. "Mark? You okay?"

"I just had this image. You handing over your real man badge and getting a wedding ring instead." His throat caught on another laugh. "Me doing the same. And a long line of men all stretched out behind us."

Eric's face crinkled into familiar laugh lines. "Should we warn our sons?"

"And spoil our fun? Nooo."

They both turned to the sound of the returning vehicles. Miguel led, stopped twenty yards away, shut off the engine. Yancey was behind him. He did the same.

"Time to go home," Eric said. "Try and convince my mother she has to stay."

"Let me know if you need help."

Mark held on to the back of the lawn chair as Eric rose. Between the two of the them, they collapsed it and side by side, struggled to their awaiting chariots.

Fate's Fourth Decision
Mark and Paulina

Prologue
Kate Wyatt, EMT

It wasn't as if she weren't prepared. The chatter on the radio made the situation clear enough: car through the guardrails, down the embankment, and into the water. That it had turned end over end and landed on its hood with its tail in the water, the back seat inhabitants near drowned if they hadn't already been dead... that little fact had not been mentioned. Probably to keep the police-scanner public off their cell phones and out of the way. Any accident brought gawkers, but a gruesome one just brought out the worst in everyone.

A gruesome, high-profile one, Kate Wyatt added to herself as she gripped one side of the gurney and tried to control her slide down the embankment without having her partner Jim plow into her. He should have gone first, purely from the weight issue, but God forbid she was going to give the man any more fodder for his misanthropic leanings. She wanted to lead? *Lead on, sister!*

Her boots slid again and she pushed backward on the gurney to balance herself. Jim grumbled an obscenity and she pushed just a little harder, catching him in the gut. Normally, she'd have smiled, but this wasn't normal.

O'Sheas. Eubanks. She heard the names from the officer at the front of the vehicle. The driver's door had been pulled open and he was crouched, leaning into it, talking in a low, soothing voice.

Angel O'Shea? Let her be alive, let her be alive, let her be alive.

Kate continued the mental prayer, moving her lips to it. Angel O'Shea had spearheaded the campaign to upgrade the equipment packages on the ambulances. What was to have been merely state-approved became state-of-the-art. Rumor had it she'd twisted each bank president around her little finger, telling A she had B's donation in pocket, then C she had B's, then back to A, confirming what he'd already heard, that B and C had given generously. She'd organized a breakfast-lunch-dinner series, each hosted by a different shift at the fire department. The public has to see what you have, what you're getting, what you *should* get she'd told the fire chief. Invite the public in, cook for them, *show* them-- then make them pay for the knowledge.

She'd raised $125,000 in less than six months and now, as Kate gently handled Paulina Eubanks from her upside down position, she tried very hard not to look in the back seat and see that all the state-of-the-art equipment in the world would not help Angel O'Shea.

Chapter 16

Ten minutes before the accident

"It handles like a thoroughbred." Paulina closed her fist around the gearshift, even though the Jag was an automatic.

Psychology 101 and phallic symbols had nothing on her, Mark thought. She could have written the book. "Careful, you'll be having..." he paused for effect and was rewarded with a shift of her eyes toward him "... car envy."

She snorted. "I expected more imagination from you than that. At the very least, Mark envy."

"Jag envy," chirped from the back seat.

"Biiigg Jag envy," was added in bass.

"Oh, puh-lease. You lot are hopeless." Paulina turned her attention back to the road.

"And we have awful imaginations at this hour," Angel said. "You'd think one of us could come up with something dirty."

"Don't know, babe. My imagination has always been very good at this hour." Mark made his voice huskier as he reached over the front console and patted Angel's leg with his left hand.

She twisted and shooed him away. "Yeah, that's right. Do I snore bass or do I snore tenor? That's as far as your imagination goes."

Eric chuckled.

"Peanut gallery." Mark straightened in his seat. "Let's ignore them, Pauli."

"You ignore them. I'm going to ignore you."

"But I'm teaching you to drive this sweet baby."

"Mark O'Shea," she started and he settled in to enjoy the words Paulina always seemed to find when he pushed her just a bit too far. It was easy to do tonight. She was tired and, for some reason known only to them--*thank God!*, she was mad at Eric. Of course her attitude would straighten up before they left for Cancun. It always had. At least by the second margarita on the beach. The second day. He tuned back in. "You couldn't even teach me to drive to distraction."

"I don't think that came out right, Paulina," Eric commented.

"Mark could drive you to drink," Angel added. "Lord knows there have been a few times…"

Paulina humphed. "I'm doing the driving. Because Mark drinks."

"I get no respect. And it's my birthday."

"*Was.*" All three of them.

"What is this, a Greek chorus?"

"Your birthday ended an hour ago."

"I turned forty-six and all I got was this lousy Jag." He smirked when he said it.

"You are hopeless. Angel, how do you put up with him?" Paulina asked to the back seat.

"Yeah, honey," Mark swiveled again to see her, "how do you put up with me?"

"I married you for your money. You know that. And since you're not worth enough yet, I just keep plugging away." Angel. Mistress of the deadpan delivery.

"Yeah, and I married Paulina for her charm."

She stiffened. *Dig that hole, Eric, just keep digging*, Mark thought, then decided to offer him a hand. "That's not what you told me," he chided, twisting to his right in order to see Eric. "You said it was for her big…" He hefted imaginary breasts.

"I was a man blinded by love. And big jugs. See, we're equal, Mark. You have a Jag, I have jugs."

The car sped up. *Are you stupid or suicidal?* Mark mouthed to his friend, who shrugged and scrunched deeper into the leather.

Mark shook his head and straightened in his seat. Okay, if Eric didn't want his help, he'd quit offering it.

***

Paulina tightened her jaw and pushed on the accelerator. It was as if the two were connected, her jaw and her foot. The more Eric talked, the more tightly wound she became, she faster she drove. Why couldn't he just shut up?

And referring to her breasts as jugs. That wasn't like Eric. What was with him tonight?

Was he jealous of the Jag? My God, she thought, how simple was that to fix? She'd let him buy a new backhoe or something.

She pulled her attention back to the road. Two-lane state highways were a bitch at night, never mind the xenon headlights cut through the dark like a hot knife. She knew Mark liked speed, but if the set of his shoulders were any indication, she was taking his new baby too fast for even his taste.

Her right foot pressed harder as they approached the bridge. It should have been rebuilt years ago, she thought, since hard curves led into it from either side of the river. The road was like a snaky-S with a big bump in the middle, the bridge being that bump. She'd taken it at 80 before. Why not again?

Why not faster?

"Pauli!" Mark's voice ripped at her ear. It was a shout, a tear in her determination. "Damn it, Pauli, slow down, there's a deer!"

And there was. Where the hell had that come from? She hit the brakes and sensed Angel and Eric shift in the back seat, felt Angel's hand grip the back of her seat. The doe bounced across, graceful, light on her four feet.

"There'll be another," Eric added from the back. Of course there would. She continued to slow, felt the collective sigh of relief as the buck followed from one side of the road to the other. At least they'd been before the curve. Once in, she'd have been hard-pressed to maintain control of the Jag.

They eased back from the sudden restraint of the seatbelts which loosened as she sped up. "Good job, Paulina," Eric whispered under his breath.

Like that was going to make up for this evening. She coaxed the car back to the speed limit. Then higher.

She liked to take this curve from this direction. Her Lexus held it well enough, but this vehicle was meant for this curve. She could sense it. She took a deep breath and pushed the accelerator harder as they entered. The compass reading on the rearview mirror changed ninety degrees.

"Pauli…" Now what was Mark complaining about? Hadn't she just pulled them out of a near disaster? "… deer!"

"Where?" Was she shrieking? What was with the animal population tonight?

There it was, another suicidal doe determined to leave the secure confines of the brush and bound across in front of her. Had their mothers not taught them to be afraid of men and cars?

She braked. Hard. But they were well into the curve. The Jag spun. Mark grabbed at the wheel to help her gain control, but there wasn't going to be any. She heard Eric and Angel in the back, their voices blended in surprise and then terror. Hers joined theirs as she hit the deer, then hit the guardrail.

They barreled down the embankment front grill first. The headlights picked out a fallen tree in their path. Hitting the brakes and turning the steering wheel proved futile, and she knew there was no hope for missing it. The front tires rammed it and the car pivoted on its nose, standing upright and then falling backwards, sliding and skidding on its top further down the embankment, rear first into the dark river.

"Oh, my God, what has happened?" She fought against the deflating airbags, sputtering and spewing and both surprised and disgruntled to find herself the only one doing so. Her head was within inches of the head space of the Jag and she realized she was hanging upside down, tethered only by her seatbelt, the muscles in her shoulders doing double duty keeping her in alignment while screaming against the confines of the harness. Beside her, Mark's forehead was bleeding onto the Jag headspace and his arms were twisted, caught in the middle between his body and the console. But he breathed.

She tried to pull her resources together. Should she attempt to unbuckle her belt, could she control her pitch into the padded roof of the Jag or would she slide into the steering wheel, the shattered front windshield? She wasn't sure if she felt her legs or not, was she curling her toes, or just thinking she was? Why was there no air to breathe?

And it was quiet. That was the most frightening of all. Water… maybe she heard water, the river rolling, slapping against the metal of the car. Maybe that was what she heard. What she didn't hear was breathing. No whimpers, no whispers.

No prayers. No hope?

She gave up the struggle to remain conscious and succumbed to blessed, blessed nothingness.

Chapter 17

Wednesday (Day of the funerals)

Mark

"**W**hat do you think you're doing?"

Yancey's voice rang through the metal building that housed Store No. 1. Mark ignored him as he continued limping toward his office. He heard the set of garage doors crash onto the concrete floor and Yancey's footsteps echo. On a normal work day, the echo was near zero. Employees were in constant motion, this place a hive of activity, as they shelved inventory and loaded trailers for contractors and do-it-yourselfers. The only echo was the sound of coins clinking in the cash register and the whiz of the credit card reader.

But that was a normal day. Today wasn't normal. He'd never know normal again.

"Mark!"

Jesus, the man was annoying. Since when could the owner not even sneak into his own business without being followed by the manager? He slammed the office door in Yancey's face.

That didn't do any good. He wasn't behind his desk

before a red-faced and visibly pissed-off Yancey was towering over him.

"What?" he asked as he fell into his desk chair. He was breathing heavily. Maybe he should have had someone drive him and stay with him, rather than slinking out his own back door and calling a taxi, dismissing the driver at the gates after he'd given him the entry code. Now he'd have to make up a new one, make sure everyone knew it. Hell, Yancey could reconfigure it and pass the word. On his way out. If the door alarm system wasn't keyed to a punch pad, he couldn't have let himself into the building. A broken left arm, a dislocated collar bone, and a severely sprained right wrist were slowing him down considerably. Not to mention the wrenched hip and the torn cartilage in his knee. They could have at least been on the same side, so his limp would have meant something, not this hitch-and-slide he might be doomed to for the rest of his life. *Crap!*

Yancey leaned onto the desk, his large hands with fingers splayed, as he balanced himself on them. "Mark O'Shea, what are you doing here?"

"I heard you the first time."

Yancey straightened up and slapped his hands on his thighs, his body language equivalent to taking off the gloves. Mark scowled, daring him to continue.

"You buried your wife this morning, your best friend two hours ago. You need to go home to your boys."

Definitely taking off the gloves.

"Shut up, Yancey." He couldn't look at the man, so he concentrated on his desk blotter, the one with the calendar and the you-are-here-Cancun sticker Angel had stuck in the middle of next week. He pulled a deep breath, but it was ragged and he knew Yancey was staring at him. He was done with tears. He was. He wasn't going to cry any more. No. He pinched his lips together and stared at the palm tree she'd sketched in for Friday, the margarita glass for Saturday and felt the first- -and *only* this time, he swore!--tear slide down his cheek. Okay, one more.

"Let me drive you home."

"It's payroll."

"I'll make out the checks and bring them over."

"They've got to be figured."

"I'll call Teresa. She'll come up and punch the right buttons on the computer. Tomorrow morning latest they'll be done. You can sign them when I bring them over."

"How did you know I was here?"

"Have you heard a word I've said?"

"How..."

"Jason called. They saw the taxi pull away from the curb and didn't want to get into it with you and they sure as hell weren't going to send your dad. Where else would you be going?"

"The bridge."

"Shit, Mark." Yancey sank into the padded client's chair. He hung his hands between his knees and shook his head. "You're not ready for that."

Maybe not, but it had made the man sit down. The words spilled from him. "What am I going to do without her?" He gave up trying to make sense out of the calendar's days off and vacation lines and instead dragged his eyes to Yancey's. "I barely remember anything in my life before she was there. We met in grade school, for chrissake. We didn't like each other, but she was always there. What am I going to do without her?" he repeated, then with a shake of his head, he voiced the fear that had nagged him since waking in the hospital on Saturday morning. "I don't know who I am without Angel."

"Oh, Mark." Yancey buried his face in his hands and rubbed his cheeks, ran his hands through his hair.

"What would you do without Franny?" Mark pestered.

"I don't think of it. Never."

"Well, you'd better. You could wake up one day and wham--it's just you!"

"Mark!" Yancey jerked his head up and stared at him. He shifted his weight, stretching his left leg under the desk and showing his discomfort with the conversation as clearly as if he had said so. "Let's get you home."

"Let's not. You need to get home--go." He would have crossed his arms on his chest and reared back if he could. He couldn't, so he just glared.

"Not going anywhere without you and I'm tired of the conversation. Don't make me call the boys."

The boys. A low blow reference if ever there was one. *Angel's angels*, she'd called them, usually when they were asleep. Especially Jason and Travis. Unexpected, life-changing babies, so close together. Unwanted, if he had to be honest about it, especially Travis. Just when they'd gotten over the shock of Jason, readjusted their lives, thought they had it figured out how they could still both make it through school, along came Travis. It had been a dark day, a dark period in their lives.

But they hadn't given up on each other. Not that he hadn't been tempted. It would have been so easy to walk out the door of the trailer and to have just kept going. She wouldn't have even come after him, although Henry Buttons would have shot him on sight. But Angel would have let him go... and let him live with the consequences of losing everything dear.

God, he had been so close to being a fool. Why had God had pity on him and made him unpack his clothes that night while she still slept? Why had God saved him then from a horrible mistake that would have changed three lives and ruined his? And why later from one that was, if anything, worse? Was this it--saved from two ill-timed mistakes so he could suffer through this agony now? Was Angel's death his punishment?

Because if it was, Eric's was Paulina's.

***

"Mom?"

Paulina raised her head from her hands as the workshop door scraped open. Her head throbbed under the bandage over her right eye. She should have known better than to bend forward and put pressure on it. Ty, his hand clutching the door knob, was silhouetted against the brightness of the late afternoon sun. Just seeing his form was seeing Eric twenty years ago.

"Yes, Ty?" She straightened, but kept her hands between her knees, her legs stretched out before her, sneakers clipped under the rim of the large drawing table. It normally held landscape plans, but she had pulled out sketches she'd never seen and covered up a rose garden and a place to be Zen. If she wasn't feeling Zen, no one was going to be Zen.

"Grandma Betty wants to know if you want anything

to drink." He shot a look at the charcoal drawings, one a portrait of two boys playing in the sand, himself and William from a vacation in Galveston, and the other of a woman standing on a balcony looking out to sea. She had a faraway look in her eye. It wasn't Paulina, but she recognized the inspiration for the look.

She pressed her lips together and shook her head. "Tell Grandma I'm fine."

"Dad was good, wasn't he?" He fingered the corner of the portrait of the boys, lifting it, letting the movement billow it until it settled back on the table.

"Yes, he was good."

"Why'd he quit?"

"Art can be difficult to make a living at." She wet her lips and felt his stare. "And we had to eat and I wasn't through law school and the landscaping business came up…" Her voice drifted off. A gallery which always took his work had closed and the portrait business was going to hell. Eric promised he'd dig in the dirt just until she got her law practice established. Then she'd taken the opportunity in the D. A.'s office and then there was Ty. Landscaping was doing far more than paying the bills and neither of them had mentioned other options for years.

"But we have money now. He could have gone back."

"Some day. He said he would some day." Eric had said that. As soon as she was making half a million a year, that's what he'd said. But he'd lied. The half-mil mark was long gone. She looked at Ty now, looked at the sketches. She hadn't known they existed. He must have come out here and done them recently, using a photo of the boys for the one and his mind's vivid eye for the other.

"Well, it's too late for that, isn't it? Some day isn't going to happen."

"Yeah." She squeezed her eyes against the tears. There were not going to be any more of them. No. No. *NO!* "I guess there's a lesson for us there. We need to take care of our *some days*."

"That's pretty philosophical, Mom."

"I'm just a philosophical gal."

He smiled. "That's sure easier than explaining that my mom beats the pants off day traders."

What did he think she did? Maybe they needed a take-your-son-to-work day that didn't involve ditches and petunias. The longer she could go and not think about Eubanks' Landscaping the better, but that was neither realistic nor feasible. *Some day* was fast approaching in that arena. She needed to call Miguel and there was the business with Yancey and Mark.

Her head was crowded. That's why she'd come out here, to clear it. And what had happened? She'd found the drawings and the beginnings of a major headache.

"How about dinner?" Ty returned to what must have been his original set of questions. "There's lots of things or Grandma Betty can make you something or Gran Melba said she'd be glad to. And," he shot a glance over his shoulder into the backyard where she could see the various family members huddled about the patio tables, drinks in hand. Laughter floated to her. No doubt they were discussing Eric's early antics--or someone's miserable golf game. Ty went back to the door and closed it, came to her again. "And I want to know when they're all leaving. We don't need them, Mom. I can take care of you."

If there had been any part of her heart and soul still whole, still not broken, it broke then. "Oh, sweetheart." That only increased the worry line across his forehead. Paulina didn't use 'sweetheart' and 'dear', didn't call him or anyone else 'honey'. Not even Eric. Not even when she should have. She reached to smooth the lines from his forehead, let her hand linger on his dark brown hair. "I know you can take care of me. We're going to take care of each other."

"So when are they leaving? They don't all have to leave, but Aunt Evie and Uncle Steve--I don't think I can take my cousins one more night." Now that he'd broached the subject, he gathered his courage and let all the frustration of the last week spill forth. "Aunt Ellen she says she's going tomorrow. And, and I don't even know who some of those people are. Where did Dad hide them? That woman Morticia--"

"Your great-aunt Hortense?"

"Whatever. She pats me every time I get near. She's Gran's age. Both of them combined. I'd go to William's, but his Grandpa Marcus is always telling us stories about the good old days. Whatever those were. Don't sound good to me."

He paused for breath.

"Are you finished?"

"Aren't you ready for them to go?" he continued to plead his case.

"I'd have been happy had they never come."

"Me, too. It's not bad enough Dad dies, we have to put up with all these strangers." He choked back a sob.

So there was a drawback to not being close to one's family, to shunning the reunions and making very quick trips at Christmas. Had they not, Ty would have been able to name all the strangers he now despised.

His tears bothered her. He'd cried at the graveside service. Paulina had forgone the ritual of a church-sanctuary funeral. Angel's was circus enough for both families. Mark had insisted she and Ty sit with the O'Sheas. She'd been sandwiched between William and Ty and found herself holding both boys' hands. It was more contact than she was used to, more than she was comfortable with, and she'd shed them--even her son's-- as quickly as she could when they stood at service's end.

The church had been standing-room-only--how many people could one family know?--and she had relished the privacy of the graveside that afternoon. Surely it would be a relief for the O'Sheas, too, to not have to endure another ordeal, just sit quietly while perfunctory words were intoned. She'd declined the offer of the double funeral. She just could not stand the idea of it. It made her jumpy and her skin crawl. Her husband was gone; she would not celebrate it.

Of course, Melba was mad at her. But not mad enough to leave, more's the pity. Ellen had tried to explain that her mother needed the funeral. Paulina told her that no one needs a funeral, especially not the sideshow which was Angel's. She was so mad at whatever God there was that Eric believed in, that the family was doing good to get any sort of formal service. She'd rather have committed him to the sea had such been within easy reach. She could have stood on the shore and shaken her fist at the heavens. Should there be a God. Should he live in the heavens. She doubted it.

And perhaps had Eric been the only one to die in the accident, it would have been different. Without the O'Shea family to be held to as comparison, she could have done what she wished and not looked bad. Angel would have stood by her and defended her from the relatives.

A smile crossed her lips.

"What's so funny, Mom?" Ty swiped at his eyes. He hadn't expected her to take him in her arms. She wasn't a cocoon like Angel was. She was a rock.

"I was thinking about Angel."

"Yeah, well, she wouldn't have put up with all this nonsense. Angel would have kicked butt and no one would ever have known it till they tried to sit down."

She didn't even try to squelch the smile and little bubble of laughter which followed it. "You're a most perceptive young man." She stood and looked him in the eye. By Christmas, she'd be looking up at him. She cupped his neck in her hands, felt the strength there, saw the sincerity in his eyes. He had all the makings of a good man if she could just finish what Eric had begun. "Well, let's go kick butt. And make sure everyone knows about it."

***

"Dad..."

"Not a word." Mark planted the crutch at the edge of the kitchen counter and boosted himself onto a bar stool. Hurt like hell, but he held his grimace in check. He couldn't be limping down the street as if he were running away from home, then pleading poor-little-me two hours later when hauled back home by Yancey. And what had Yancey done? Oh, yeah. Some friend. He'd pulled to the O'Shea back entrance, leaned across the man who signed his checks, flipped open the door, and not waved good-bye when Mark had finally struggled out. "I'll have a Scotch."

Jason shook his head. "Not on your meds."

"You're not a doctor yet."

"Dad." He pinched the bridge of his nose and stared at his feet. William was no where to be found, Travis was glaring at him from the table in the breakfast area, and Marcus was assembling a drink. For whom was anyone's guess, but Mark would bet he wasn't getting any. "You can't mix medicine and alcohol just now. Maybe in a week you'll be off the meds."

A trick he learned from Angel, no doubt. It should make him a fine doctor, but his believability on the son-level was going steadily downhill. Hold out that carrot with a little bit of hope strung to the end. *Not today, Dad. Not tomorrow. But next week. You can make it until next week, can't you, Dad?*

No. Especially not in the armed camp that had set up in his house. Last Saturday, Delores and Henry Buttons took over the den for their headquarters. She had insisted they not put any of the boys out of their rooms, although he knew William was sleeping in Travis's other bunk bed. Each morning this week Henry had suggested they return home, and Delores claimed they needed her in the kitchen, if no where else. Truth be told, Mark had to admit he preferred his mother-in-law's cooking, which was so similar to Angel's, to that of his own mother. Iona had showed up the day before the funeral, all sad smiles and hugs, regrets dripping from her lips because she'd been on a cruise and hadn't heard the awful, awful news until she returned home. Once Iona had crossed the threshold, he knew there was no way Delores was going until she did. Delores was there to protect her daughter's interests, and even grief would not keep her from it.

Angel's sisters, however, were a different matter. How one family could produce three such disparate daughters was beyond his ken. Unashamedly, two days ago, he had looked from their suitcases to Delores and had let a tear fall from his eye and slither down his cheek. Delores had warped from protecting her territory into protecting him, and the sisters had gone to a motel. It was the first time in all the years of his marriage, that he could have genuinely told his mother-in-law he loved her.

But enough of that sentimental crap. The funeral was over. Angel's things--her clothes, her jewelry, her hair brush for God's sake--were a source of great consternation for both mothers. What was it with women that they wanted to clean up the dead so quickly? Delores had even hinted that Angel's sisters might like a small memento of Angel's. She'd said it with a smile, but all Mark could think of was the diamond tennis bracelet the funeral home had handed him along with her twenty-fifth anniversary ring. How dare Delores? How *dare* she?

And now Iona was standing on one side of his kitchen and Delores, sans Henry who had had the sense to leave last night, had entered through the back door. She carried two sacks of groceries and William--how desperate was the boy to leave the house for him to go with his grandmother any where?--followed with two more. There was a war brewing, and Marcus wasn't making anyone a drink but himself. With weary eyes, Mark followed his father's progress around the table and through the French doors to the pool. He set the drink on the paving stones and eased himself to a sit, placing his feet in the water and visibly sighing.

Mark could have killed. His own feet were encased in boots to help him walk. He wanted a drink. Jason just thought he knew about pain.

His protest was stopped by his mother. "Really, Delores, a trip to the store wasn't necessary. I'd think there'd be enough here for weeks. We can freeze the casseroles in proper portion size." Like Iona had any idea what a proper portion was. She had skidded between waif and heifer for years.

"Then how fortunate I've bought just the thing." Delores smiled sweetly and started to dig out disposable containers from the sacks. The battle lines had just been drawn and he was on Delores's side. That woman knew a proper portion when she saw it. Not only were the containers of the quart variety, she'd stayed a proper heifer size ever since he'd known her.

He was going to Hell, he was going to Hell, he was going to Hell. Mark hung his head and shook it. Travis got up from the table and put his arms around him from the back. He was shaking, his face buried between Mark's shoulder blades. *God, son, don't cry, don't break down in front of this assembly.* He twisted on the stool to take the young man in his arms, only to find the shaking caused not by tears, but laughter.

Once found out, Travis exploded with it, backing into a stool and causing it to tumble into the next one. A domino effect, with the next three crashing into the window, but not breaking it. He couldn't have handled a broken window just now. But the domino effect was something else. As soon as Travis started, Jason caught on. William, still uncertain of the territory, joined in only when Mark found himself unable to control the laughter. He clung to his second son and tears streamed down their faces.

"Mom," Jason started and had to stop he was laughing so hard, "Mom wouldn't freeze a thing because she knows you're too lazy to thaw it!"

"That's a lie," he retorted with mock indignation. "I'll have William do it for me."

"Which is precisely why I think I should stay on," Iona stated.

The laughter died, like water from a tapped-out spigot. Shut off abruptly.

There was panic in William's eyes. Did it match his own? "Mother..." Mark started.

"I'll thaw and cook." William scrambled to get between his grandmothers. He took the chicken casserole from Iona and grabbed a spatula from the drawer. Measuring the size of the plastic container with his hand, he cut a slice the approximate size, deposited it in the box, snapped the lid shut and reached for the permanent marker in the pen can. "Chicken," he said out loud as he wrote. "June." He looked from one woman to the other. "Don't need the year because we clean everything out once a year and the month is sufficient plus this was good. Real good. It'll be gone in a week." To prove his point he opened the freezer door and popped it in.

He turned to his grandmothers. Hands on hips, he was the picture of Angel in full battle mode, heavy breathing and all. "We can take care of ourselves, Grandma Delores, Grandma Iona. We can. Dad and I'll take care of each other. And you can call and check on us, but, but we'll be fine." He glanced over at Mark for approval but Mark was stunned. "You have to go home now. Both of you. We love you. But you have to go home."

Stunned and extremely proud.

***

"I expected more from you, Mom." Ty shook his head. "That was not Paulina Eubanks in her best kick-butt form."

Everyone was a critic.

"What would you have had me do?" She sat on the edge of her bed and pulled off first one sneaker, then the other. Her feet hurt. Her head hurt. If her son, who had followed her to her sanctuary like a hound on the scent, had anything to say about it, her pride was going to hurt. "Gather their suitcases and put them by the front door?"

"You think that would work? I'll go do it." He turned and was halfway to the closed bedroom door before she thought to stop him.

"Hortense is leaving in the morning. Ellen, Evie and Steve are packing as we speak. And were before we came in to the house. Melba can't seem to pull herself together." Was that everyone? No. "Mom and Dad think we still need them." And maybe she did. Maybe, in some sort of this-is-how-you-make-up-to-me-for-my-miserable-childhood way, she still did need them. She needed them to show her they weren't the sycophants she knew them to be.

"What we're going to be needing is more booze. Granddad is putting it away like water. The expensive stuff!" he hissed.

"We only have expensive stuff." She rubbed her feet and eased onto the bed, pulling herself to rest against the pile of pillows stacked at the head. Just because there were no bones broken inside her, and the MRI said she was okay, did not make her muscles any less sore. She had hung upside-down, as had all of them. Upside-down until hands had gently moved her, awakened her back to consciousness, until arms had lifted her, unbuckled her seat belt, strapped her onto a stretcher. Flown her away in a chopper. Her first helicopter ride and she'd been under an oxygen mask. Perhaps she would be better off if she openly bore the signs of the accident like Mark did.

Perhaps she wouldn't feel so guilty.

A third deer, half a mile from the other two. Had there been a fourth? It didn't matter; it was a moot point anyway. Moot to everyone but Angel and Eric.

She had to get back to work, had to find her sanity in the only place she was sure it still existed. She looked at Ty, standing at the foot of the bed, his face crest-fallen in that she had not given a proper battle and had taken no prisoners. Instead, they were the prisoners, trapped inside their home with jailers she thought she'd escaped a lifetime ago.

"I'm going to William's."

Not even the respect to ask. Not that he usually did. The rule was that they were to know at all times where he was. And so she would know. But she'd never been so hurting. So alone.

But he hurt too. He was alone, too. Lost. He could more easily bury himself in his friends. She... she had one real friend and she'd killed her.

She blinked the tears away and pasted a wan smile on her face. "Good. We need a report from the other side. And if all their relatives are gone, I want to know how they did it."

Chapter 18

Paulina already knew the nights would be the worst.

At night there would be no place to hide, no phone calls to return, no research to do on a spurious stock tip one of her clients was demanding she pursue. She couldn't stay at the office all night. She wouldn't break her rule and bring her work home. Just because Eric was dead did not mean this house was not a home. For Ty, it was all he knew. For her, it was the culmination of a dream, and like all her dreams, she'd pushed and pushed for its fruition.

Absently she stroked Ruffles' fur. The old cat had followed her up the stairs after she'd made her excuses and left her parents in the kitchen. She was tired of making nice and she'd ignored the in-laws at the pool. Ty had not come home from William's, but he had called. It looked to be interesting at the O'Shea's. They were laughing.

Good God, what about?

And speaking of the deity, what made him good anyway? Even had she been an avid believer, she'd have been pissed beyond bearing at this turn of events.

Chewing on the tip of her left thumb, a despicable habit she'd finally ditched when she could afford biweekly manicures, she stood at the bedroom window overlooking the driveway. A week ago, Mark had pulled his pride and joy Jag in and dared her to not like it, to not congratulate him. Hell, she could afford a Jag, she'd wanted to tell him. But he knew that. He knew a lot of things.

He knew too many things.

But he didn't know that a few hours later her husband had accused her of not loving him anymore. Why had he picked that night, that dance? Could he not have waited until Cancun? Could he not have just kept his mouth shut and waited for her to come back to him?

You'll regret marrying an artist. That's what Aunt Hortense had told her at a wedding shower. *They're too perceptive by far and you'll never get away with a thing.* Maybe that was why she'd avoided the old girl all these years. She hadn't wanted to admit that while Hortense wasn't right, she had at least had a point.

Disappointment clouded their marriage. It was a burden to be married to a good man who would sacrifice his dream and talent in order for her to pursue hers. Ego had nothing to do with it. It was Eric's perception of the right thing to do. The *damned* right thing to do. Then when she was quite capable of taking over the finances, of leaving him to follow his artist again, he wouldn't. Too many people counted on him, he said, too many good, hard-working people, none of whom had the vision he did. Or the resources. And besides, he liked what he did. There would be time for art later.

If that wasn't a take-home lesson in doing today instead of putting off to tomorrow, she didn't know what was.

It irritated her when he came in as dirty as she knew his crews were. Digging trenches, shoveling manure, hauling brick… if the job needed to be done, he did it. Which is why his crews adored him, why there had been a steady stream of visitors to the funeral home, names scrawled in the guest book that were familiar only because she'd seen them in the checkbook. Her kitchen was redolent of a fine Mexican restaurant, and her mother had had to turn off the phone to end the offers of help.

And she was surely the most ungrateful bitch Eric's God had ever created.

She'd called Miguel and tomorrow he would be here before noon. They needed to figure out what to do about the business because surely the vision existed for someone now. They'd work out some sort of deal. She didn't like loose ends and uncertainty and here was one part of her life that she could sort out if not easily, then at least in a timely manner.

But she'd still be alone.

***

Mark held his head with two fingers massaging his forehead, the thumb digging into his cheek. His left elbow rested on the arm of his favorite den lounger, "that piece of crap", as Angel was fond of noting. It no longer went with the décor, a piece of stubbornness on both their parts when she'd redecorated three years ago. The chair was molded to his body. Why should he give it up?

But that argument was long gone and never to be revived and was not the current cause of his consternation. William and Ty stood before him. "Why not, Dad? Ty stays over here all the time."

"Ty needs to go home to his mother."

"But I got all my grandparents there and the aunts and uncle and the smothering is about to kill me, Mark."

Mark quirked a brow. Realizing his choice of words for what they were, the boy squatted on the floor in front of him. "I'm sorry, Mark. I didn't mean kill. They won't hurt me. And they'll be gone tomorrow. And so will I from here."

"Go home to your mother. You think she wants to be alone?"

"She's no more alone than you are."

Ty's frustration was nearing boiling, but Mark had no sympathy.

"You have no idea how alone we are, son."

"C'mon, Ty." Jason peeled himself off the door jamb and strode across the floor. He touched the boy on the shoulder. "I'll give you a ride home."

Ty jerked away from him. "I can get home by myself."

Jason held his hands up and stepped away. "If you think you're the only one that's hurting…"

"Take it elsewhere," Mark intervened. He pulled himself forward in the chair and struggled to stand. "Ty, go home. William, help your grandmothers carry out the garbage. Jason and Travis, you can stay or leave. I'm going up."

"Dad, I'll help you." Travis scrambled off the couch and leapt to Mark's side.

He waved him off. "Who's helping me upstairs when you leave, huh?"

"William."

The boy came to his own defense. "Yeah, that's right. William's here. William can do it!"

The tempers were about to flare. Too much testosterone had been Angel's answer for every argument under this roof. She'd no sooner complain than be playing the queen bee in this hormone-soaked hive. But this wasn't too much testosterone; this was too much grief, grief they couldn't direct elsewhere. If Eric hadn't died, the O'Sheas would have had the Eubanks to lean on. They wouldn't have decompensated like this. Eric would have been the brother Marshall refused to be, even to the point of calling the night before Angel's service to say he was sorry but he couldn't come. Paulina would have taken over the O'Shea house, stood as sentry between his boys and himself and the outside world, even the relatives that threatened to unhinge his life. Paulina would have taken charge and he would have let her, gratefully allowed it, because she would have fought for them, even while Ty said she wasn't fighting in her own domain now.

But that was all speculation. Reality was before him, his three sons and a boy almost as much his, ready to square off. He could let his own have at it, but Ty wasn't equipped to fight this horde, with William or in his own defense.

"I tell you what." He turned, trying not to grimace. "Jason and Travis, you pack up and leave tonight. You have school and work. You're useless here. Come back next weekend. The sooner the grandmothers figure there's no one to take care of, the sooner they'll leave us be. Ty, you go home. William, you go with him. I've had it with all of you." He limped over to the stairs. "I mean it, boys," he said to the air in front of him, "go now."

Their footsteps were silent, and there were no protests. He concentrated on the steps in front of him, each of them looming large, Angel's perfect "rise over run" theory of stairs showing him little mercy as he put his weight on the hand rail and pulled himself up. It took ten minutes to get to his bed, and he fell backwards across it, fully clothed, crying like he hadn't in years.

***

Paulina raised her head from the pillow at the knock on the door. What did her mother want now? "Yes?" she answered feebly.

The door cracked open and Ty stuck his head in. "Just wanted you to know I'm back." He opened the door wider once he saw she was dressed. "And William's with me." She could see him behind Ty.

"Okay. Just don't make too much noise."

He didn't close the door, didn't leave her alone. There was something else.

"What do you need, Ty?"

The boys exchanged looks and took cautious steps into her room. She pushed herself to a sitting position and swiped the hair off her face. If she still had any make-up on, it would be gathered in the corner of her eyes and below, giving her the appearance of a raccoon. She didn't care. "Well, boys?" Had something happened between the two houses?

"Mark kicked us out."

"Because…" This was worse than dealing with uncooperative witnesses in court.

"I think he's just tired of it all," William answered. "He made Travis and Jason go home and the

211

grandmothers are setting up camp to see who gets to stay and take care of us. I think they may fight, Paulina."

He was so earnest, so worried. With his brows drawn together and his lips pursed, he was the image of Angel in concentration. As if Delores and Iona would actually, physically... Paulina paused in her thoughts. She was well acquainted with Delores, while Iona remained a shadowy figure spoken little of by Mark or Angel. But she could see Delores getting ready to defend her territory.

"Hmmm." She certainly couldn't criticize. Melba and Betty were equally contentious. "I don't know what to say about that, William. You're welcome to stay here, but I fear you're just exchanging one set of battling senior citizens for another."

"Dad'll want me home tomorrow. He didn't make me take Dweeb so he'll be even more tired of him."

She nodded. "That works. Just be quiet and don't disturb anyone. Now goodnight."

They didn't move. She cocked a brow and Ty ran over to her, gave her a quick kiss on the cheek and then they both left, gently clicking the door as they did.

She raised her hand to her cheek. Ty didn't kiss her goodnight or good morning, barely acknowledged her sometimes. This sudden display of affection, this need for her to be here and be real... A tear slipped down her cheek. What was she going to do?

She stayed like that, sitting on the edge of the bed, one hand pressed to her cheek until her cell phone rang. Who would be doing that?

Why had she left it on in the first place?

Curiosity made her rise and stumble to the vanity stool where her purse was tossed. She pulled it out and read the Caller-ID. Mark.

They hadn't talked privately since the accident. She'd seen him in the hospital, at the funeral home, at the services. It was as if they'd had an unspoken agreement not to contact each other. She flipped the device open.

"Mark?"

"Did the boys make it over?"

"Yes." She went back to the bed and sank onto it. "They said you kicked them out."

"I did. What else did they say?"

"That there's about to be a battle royale for kitchen dominance."

"And I'm sure that's how it was phrased."

A smile crossed her lips. "Precisely. They're well-read boys."

"Comics and gamer instructions."

"No, Mark. They're male. They don't read instructions."

There was a chuckle. "So, Pauli, are you feeling better?"

"Is there a better, Mark?"

"There has to be. I'd hate to think this was as good as it was ever going to get again."

"How are your injuries?" There were so many, she knew she couldn't catalog them.

"I'm stiff and sore and pissed."

"What are you pissed about?"

"What am I not?"

"True enough."

It was good to hear his voice, good to know he wasn't any better off mentally and spiritually than she was. Which was such a selfish thing. With his injuries, she should at least be wishing him a speedier recovery in the spiritual department.

If there were a God, she was surely on his shit-list now.

And she might never deserve to be off it.

"Pauli, it's none of my business, but…"

"Go on, Mark." She knew what was coming. Didn't he have a right to know, a right to know what had put her in such a snit she was driving like a madwoman?

"Pauli…" He kept hesitating. Was she going to have to just tell him? "The night of the accident… you weren't drinking, were you?"

"Oh, Mark." He'd taken her breath away with a totally unexpected question. "You know I don't. That I never…" Tears threatened, giant drops, picked up by her eyelashes and splashed across her cheeks. "They had so many blood samples from me I felt like a pincushion." She fought to control her voice. "How can you even ask?"

His voice broke. "Pauli, I had to. I know you don't drink. But that night you and Eric were so upset with each other. You can't blame me for wanting to hear it from you."

It was my car. It was my wife. It was my best friend. He didn't have to say all those things, she heard them in her head, her heart. "I'm sorry, Mark," and before she could blubber anything else, she closed the phone and tossed it into Eric's recliner beside the bed.

***

Jesus H. Christ, just take him out and shoot him right now.

The last thing he wanted to do was hurt Pauli any

more than she already was, but didn't he have a right to know?

Of course, they'd tested her for alcohol. Standard operating procedure at an accident. And if there'd been any, wouldn't he have known it, wouldn't he have been told? But he had to ask, he had to have her tell him.

And he'd chickened out on the real question: Why were you and Eric fighting?

What if, after all these years…

No, he wouldn't think about it. It was too unbearable to think about anyhow. That would have just been the last straw, if Eric knew. If Eric had always known.

Mark shut his eyes, pressed his lips together, and shuddered. The bedroom was suddenly stifling and his heart raced. Panic attack? High blood pressure? Maybe Jason hadn't left yet. Or perhaps he could just take a couple of deep breaths and sneak down to the liquor cabinet.

Nah, he couldn't do that. Besides, a man with his physical impairments didn't sneak anywhere. He eyed the cell phone still clutched in his hand. Should he call her back?

It would just make matters worse. He needed to sleep, not that he'd be getting any. There were no comfortable positions.There was no shutting off his mind. What if he just let it roam rather than trying to shut it down?

His eyes strayed to Angel's bedside table. A tour guide on Mexico was beside the alarm clock. Now why would she need that when they never left the complex and they'd been to the same one for years? He heaved himself off his side the bed and inched around to hers, supporting himself with one hand on the mattress. Even that was easier than scooting across the bedspread to the other side. It was a new book. Maybe she was looking to shop. He picked it up and carried it to the bench at the foot of the bed. The hard surface was easier for him to get up from and he sat down. Maneuvering the book with both hands, he let the pages fall apart. She'd marked the Restaurante Hildalgo. They'd eaten there once. The first year. The year Paulina lost her top in the water.

The year he'd decided to make a complete and utter fool of himself.

Did Angel know? Was that why it was marked? Did she want to return to the scene of his crime of foolhardy passion?

He had to know. He reached for his cell and punched redial.

"What, Mark?" Her voice was constricted, as if she'd been crying. Pauli didn't cry. Not even...

"Come get me."

"What?" That wasn't constricted.

"You heard me. I can't sleep and I know damn well you can't either. So come get me."

"Let's do this in the morning. Whatever this is."

"What this is is I can't drive and you can. We got to do this, Pauli. Come get me. By the time you get here I can struggle out to the front steps."

"And where do you suggest we go?"

"Your office."

"You have lost your mind."

"What's wrong with your office?"

"I haven't been there in a week."

"All the more reason it'll look natural you're there now."

"With companion. Late at night."

"I'm not going to play this game. Come get me."

"I should call your housemothers and get them to lock you in."

A smile twitched at the corner of his mouth. She was hooked. "I dare you."

Silence.

"Okay. Not enough of a challenge? Double dare you."

"All right, Mark. I'll be there. But I'm not coming in after you. And I'm not helping you into the car. If--"

"Cool your jets. You get here and I'll get in."

Chapter 19

"**I** cannot believe I've let you talk me into this." Paulina unlocked the door to her suite of offices and held it open for Mark to limp through. The table lamp in the client area had been left on, and her eyes swept over the neatened desktops, the computers ready for the next day. The carpet was vacuum cleaner marked and the wastebaskets empty, so the cleaning staff had already been in. Good. The chances of a witness to this debacle just went down.

"Turn on the lights so I don't complete the job of permanent disability," Mark growled as he continued on his lop-sided way to her personal office at the back of the suite. She sighed and locked the front door, flipping the main light switch in one smooth motion. He hadn't said a word on the trip over, just hunched in the front seat of her Lexus, refusing to wave to Delores and Iona as they stood in their robes at the front door. And Mark had thought to sneak out of the house? God knew what *they* thought.

If God was concerned with any of this, he shouldn't have let it happen.

She followed Mark, amazed to find him already at her locked door. "What is this," he continued with the grousing, "locking the inner sanctum?"

"It's a security measure. Keeps out the casual night visitor."

He snorted. "Computer theft is all that counts nowadays." He followed her in and promptly fell into the closest chair, let the crutches fall with a soft thud to the carpet. "And you sit over on this side with me. None of this behind the desk I'm-the-boss crap."

"All the I'm-the-boss crap I know, I learned from you." She pulled the brass chain on the green-shaded desk lamp, a relic from a library white elephant sale. She and Angel had made out like bandits that day, supplying each desk in either house with an antique, green-shaded lamp.

"And you excelled as only the best student can."

"Mark." She eased into the other client chair. The urge to get behind her desk, to get into the computer files, see where the office stood, what had happened in the last week, that urge was almost overpowering. She had thought she could control it, that it wouldn't come close to consuming her, but it did. She gripped the armrests and glared at him. Tomorrow she'd come in on her own.

Tomorrow. She just had to make it through whatever denouement or accusation Mark had in mind tonight, kick his butt out at his curb, and then come back.

Tonight. Because she wasn't going to get any sleep.

She primly crossed her legs at the ankle and folded her hands in her lap.

"You're not going to help me here, are you?"

"If I knew where you needed help, perhaps I could."

She tweaked the corner of her mouth. "Not that I would."

"Glad to know your mouth wasn't injured." He shifted his weight, grimaced.

She felt sorry for him but moved only to clasp her hands together more tightly.

"Okay, Pauli, it's like this." He balanced his good elbow on the armrest and leaned into it, pinched his lips together before licking them and continuing. "Did Eric know?"

"Did Eric know what?" She measured her words, knew very well what he meant.

"About us."

"There isn't any us."

"Not now."

"Not ever again."

"Did he know about us--then?"

"No."

"You're sure?"

"Mark, why are you asking?"

"Then what were you fighting about?" He straightened in the chair. "And don't bother denying it. You were in the middle of some cat snit and it wasn't about picking up the laundry or whose turn it was to do the dishes. Not any secret you were upset when you traipsed into the bar like you did. What did Eric forget?" He settled his eyes on her white-knuckled hands, and she quickly forced them apart and crossed her arms. He raised his eyes to hers. "Or what did he remember?"

"That's none of your business."

"You think not?" His voice raised. "My wife's dead! My life is in the toilet and you're walking around without a scratch on you and it's *none of my business why*?"

"Mark!" How *dare* he?

220

"Pauli, I got a right to know." He slumped back in the chair and when he spoke again his voice was little more than a whisper. "Angel had a tour book beside the bed and it was marked at the Restaurante Hildalgo. You know…"

"I know."

"I can't stand the thought she knew. After all these years if she knew."

"And you honestly think she wouldn't confront you?"

He shook his head. "She'd never ask. She'd just forgive."

"You're deifying the dead."

"You're forgetting…"

"I'm forgetting nothing. Look, Mark, she took that Mexican cooking course in February and she remembered we'd had some dish with shrimp and peppers and she wanted to go back and taste it again or beg the recipe or something. She asked me if I remembered the name of the restaurant because she couldn't."

"And of course you remembered."

"I forget very little."

"Except what you and Eric were fighting about."

"You're like a damn dog with a bone."

"Then help me bury this one somewhere other than between my shoulder blades."

"That is an ugly picture."

"Quit thinking and start talking."

"I don't know what Eric knew." He started to protest and she raised her hand to stop his words. "He told me he knew I didn't love him. Least not like I should. Like I did."

He stared at her.

"What?" She drew back in mock surprise. "I can't believe it. I finally said something that stopped that flood of nonsense from your mouth."

"That was it? Out of the blue he accuses you of not loving him? *Now*?"

"Now."

"Is there someone else?"

Paulina felt her cheeks blaze, her inner thermometer rise exponentially as she repeated the words to herself, then found some of her own. "How dare you ask." She shot out of the chair and headed to the open door. "You have two minutes to get your ass to my car. After that, you may rot here all night." Her fist curled around the door knob.

"That's not an answer, Pauli. I could make a case for yes or no."

She clenched her teeth. "Get up, Mark. We're going!"

"You won't leave me here. What would the office staff say in the morning? I mean, we were always worried about that. What would people say?"

"Trust me in that I am far less worried about it now than I was seven years ago."

He shook his head. "Not you, Paulina. You'll always be worried about what people think. You've got this high bar set for yourself and you don't want to fall off it. Having an affair with me was about as close to teetering as you ever came."

She slumped into the door frame. "Why are we doing this, Mark? It was over almost as quickly as it began and no one the wiser. Angel might have forgiven but Eric never. If he knew, he'd have said so right out. Please, can we just go home?"

"And sin no more?"

"I have no intention of sinning with you or anyone else."

"Because to sin you'd have to believe in someone who set you an even higher bar."

"Goodnight, Mark." She closed the door on him and flipped the lights off in the main office as she left.

***

Mark sat in the vacant office and listened to the tick of the clock on the credenza. He didn't think clocks still did that, that batteries had taken care of all the ticking. He let his eyes rove over to it, to the curved case and the gold hands. It was old, not imitation of antique but the genuine article. Of course she would have it here. He remembered when Paulina and Angel had found it in the shed that passed for an antique shop in some ski village in Colorado.

Angel had wanted it, had probably spied it first, pointed it out to Pauli to admire. But something about it had called to Paulina and before Angel could lay claim, she had. Most expensive twenty-five dollars he'd ever spent, Eric told him later, what with the trips into Dallas to find the appropriate clockmaker, the lunches and shopping trips that accompanied them. Fixing the clock was in the hundreds. The attendant expense hit the high four figures, if you counted the weekend the two families spent there when she went to get it.

Now he got to sit here for the rest of the night and listen to it. He could make it to the leather couch, but he doubted he'd be able to get off of it. So in the morning he'd get to explain it all to the security people. He would need a good night's sleep.

Or she might get halfway home and decide to take pity on him, come back for him. He'd haul his ass out of the chair and go if she did. No more questions because there weren't going to be any answers.

That first summer in Cancun, he'd been a fool. Something in Paulina had always aroused his spirit, usually his fighting spirit. It was as if topics just appeared at random and they'd immediately hop on different sides. So when she'd lost her top in the surf, he'd thought to have a good laugh--and a good look. It didn't matter she was his best friend's wife, his wife's best friend; he was a man and men looked.

But at dinner that night, he'd excused himself to go to the men's room. She must have excused herself right after because they met in the narrow hall to the kitchen, had been pushed together by a waiter with a laden tray. He'd reached to shield her, pushed her against the wall, touched her breast, she'd turned to him, their lips just an inch apart and God help him, he'd felt the zing of attraction. Mutual attraction.

He'd had to know. He'd pursued her into dark corners and through whispered conversations, clandestine calls in the car, pursued her until he knew she'd felt that zing also.

Then they'd acted on that zing, met at a hotel in Dallas. He'd never been so scared.

The affair didn't last through the autumn. But while it had… he'd been a different man, a man he never wanted to be again. He'd felt hunted, exhilarated, ashamed, free. If Angel or Eric had ever found out…. He'd hugged his sons extra tight that Christmas, been extra generous.

Extra grateful.

The door snapped open and Paulina stood there, the office dark behind her. "Are you coming or not?"

He bent over and picked up his crutches. He held them together in front of himself, leaned his head on their length. "Can't we just finish this now? It would seem like a logical thing to do. I'm here. You're here. I can't sleep. You can't…"

Paulina cut him off with a slam of the door. She watched the involuntary jump of his shoulders. Sitting back down in front of him, she clasped her hands between her knees and set her jaw, then snapped her head up to stare at him. "Sure. Let's finish this. Although I don't know what the hell else there is to say, Mark. Seven years ago we were fools walking a tightrope. We had an affair. It was brief, torrid, and extremely tawdry. We were lucky to escape with our marriages intact and then somehow--because our spouses were oblivious to our depression and bad moods--somehow, we all stayed friends. I don't know what drew us together. There's been many a time since then that I've shaken my head in dismay. What did I see in you that was worth risking my marriage for?"

"Well, let's just take off the gloves, shall we?"

"We've never worn gloves, Mark. You and I were always hands-on."

"That's right." His hands clenched and reddened on the crutches. "Those were your hands all over me at the Sheraton."

"One would have thought you'd have chosen a less well-known hotel."

"One would have been wrong. You weren't a no-tell motel sort. Couldn't have you going home with flea bites."

He was picking a fight. The realization straightened Paulina's back and she started calculating the why of it. The whys. There were so many reasons why he would want to fight with her. A dead wife. A totaled Jag. A ruined family.

And he could blame them all on her. So he was picking a fight.

She could rise to the occasion or not, but Paulina Eubanks never backed down.

"If I recall correctly--and I do--you said you loved me."

Low blow. They'd said a great many things to each other and those words had come out of his mouth but once. She, on the other hand, had never replied in kind.

A smile etched his features. "That's right, Pauli. For one brief moment, I lost my head. I'd say it was to get you in bed with me but I think you were already there."

She raised her eyebrows for him to continue.

"Under me. You were under me at the time."

"You do have a good memory."

"That's not all you said was good."

True enough. But… there was either a subject he didn't want to broach or was dying to and wouldn't do it himself.

So she would. "We wished our spouses gone." She gave a slight shrug, watched his face closely. "Maybe not dead. But gone. So we could be together. We were that deluded, that besotted with each other. Just another textbook case of opposites attracting." She paused. "And then burning themselves out." His face clouded over. This is what he wanted to discuss. This was the reason for the meandering. Guilt. "And now Eric and Angel are gone."

"Do you feel guilty, Pauli?"

"I feel hollow, Mark. There's nothing left to me." How much brutal honesty did he want? "Seven years ago we gave in to a cosmic temptation. We said things that would have mentally killed our spouses and physically shot our marriages and families to hell and back. I still don't know why we did it. Were we bored? Did we feel unloved, unfulfilled? Did we need a little spice in the romance department, a little danger with the sex, something to ramp it up? Something to make us feel again?"

"Covering old ground. If we weren't fucking we were discussing why we wanted to."

"This is new ground with new rules, a new playing field and you know it. And you're scared. Just like I am. Two months from now if we go to dinner together, nobody says a thing, but 'look at the friends who are grieving together. Maybe they can comfort each other.' And in a year if we married, we'd have the world's blessing. It's what we said we wanted once upon a time, but right now, Mark, I can think of no more abhorrent and damning thought." She stood and looked down on him. "I'm fighting no more tonight. Let's go."

He turned soulful eyes on her. "It's all I can do to be here with you, Pauli, to look at you and not scream inside for Angel. I feel so guilty, never mind I haven't had a wayward thought or touch toward you since we came to our senses." He drew a deep breath. "Or shortly thereafter. But I'm guilty because I'm alive. And you're part of that." He pulled himself up on his crutches and balanced to get them under his arms. She didn't offer help, and he didn't ask for any.

She turned the desk lamp off and the office overheads

on. They rode home in the same silence they'd held on their way to her office. Twenty minutes later she left him at his well-lit doorstep, secure in the knowledge that Delores and Iona waited on the other side of the drawn curtains.

She returned to work and didn't leave until noon.

Epilogue
Fate's Final Decision
One week later

Damn, damn, damn. Mark balanced himself between his crutches and surveyed the broken guardrail. He dug the rubber tips into the gravel and swayed slightly. *Down there.* Down there, just a week ago, it had almost ended. Everything gone. To not see his sons again, to not hold his wife... He shuddered. Could he have handled the situation any better than Paulina? Sober, of course. Cold, stone sober. Two deer, yes, but a third further down the road? Probably not. He'd have done the same thing. Once past the presumed danger, he'd have given into that same temptation and borne down on the gas. They would have still ended up in the water, upside down and praying.

He was a good dad, he knew he was. He'd enjoyed fatherhood once the shock of the unexpected passed. And the diapers. And the teen years. Except there was still William. His punishment for thinking he'd broken the good daddy code? He'd just have to redouble his efforts. At his age, everything was harder. And now this. He might not be permanently crippled, but he was surely humbled.

Now someone was breaking into his peace. He didn't turn as approaching footsteps crunched on the gravel at the highway's edge. Instead, he longed to be able to stuff his hands in his pockets and jingle the change. It was what Mark O'Shea did when he was nervous or tired or waiting. Today, he was all three and he fixed his eyes on a spot just beyond the line of crushed bushes. Maybe whoever it was would go away.

"How the hell did you get here?"

Mark cast a sidelong glance at Eric. "Yancy. I'll call him, tell him my new chauffeur has shown up."

"Fair enough. But *why* are you here?"

"Needed to talk to God. Straighten out a few things. What's your excuse?"

"Thought I'd try the same thing."

"Does Pauli know?"

"That I'm here or that I've taken to communing with the Almighty?"

"I figure if she knows one, she knows the other." Mark turned back to study the drop to the river. His eyes swept over the broken saplings, the tire marks in the sand by the water's edge. So many impressions--and too many memories--remained. He shook the thought of red lights and radio squawk from his mind. The thwack of helicopter blades held new meaning for him and he wouldn't hear them again without chills.

Had it only been a week? Without thinking, he rolled his neck and stretched his shoulders, twisted and whipped as the Jag bounced and slid down the embankment. The tightening of the seatbelt, the explosion of the airbags... He was bruised in places he didn't know he had and the slightest movement caused pain and draw a moan from deep in his throat, an expulsion of breath he had trouble retrieving.

"Could be that if God knows all, Paulina does too." Eric tested the remaining rail, then half-sat, half-leaned against it, gingerly balancing himself between highway necessity and a cane. His eyes swept down the embankment and he slowly shook his head, as his throat started to close up. It was little more than a whisper. "I cannot believe we survived that."

Mark nodded. "They hauled the Jag up Monday. Neely says I'll have a check next week."

Eric shook his head and laughed ruefully as his lungs started to cooperate once more. "Going to get another one?"

"Think I'll get a Hummer with two rollover bars and radar. Maybe sonar, too. And I'll not be letting your wife near it."

"I heard that."

"I heard that." The phrase echoed. Eric jerked his head around, immediately winced at the sharp pain diving down his spine. Who had said that at the same time he did? Who else would but Paulina? She had to be directly behind them, and they'd not heard her approach. Note to self: get another hearing test.

Eric swiveled toward her, but the movement cost him as his ribs protested. Why had he thought he could make it out here on his own?

"You wearing mufflers on your feet now?" Mark asked without looking at her.

"Don't be snide, Mark." Paulina fitted herself between them and took Eric's upper arm, clutching it to herself and stepping closer to him, her chin resting on his head. It was a cozy, you're-mine stance and he circled her linen-clad hips with one arm. He closed his eyes to savor a closeness experience told him would not last through the summer. But then, everything had changed for them, hadn't it? You couldn't survive what they had without wondering why, without wondering if things were meant to be better. *Had* to be better. "You were deep in thought," she said, and he felt the vibration in her throat. "A rare occurrence. For both of you." She stroked his other arm, nails sending shivers to his center. Now how could she still do that? "I cannot believe we survived." It was barely more than a whisper.

"I entered you in the next demolition derby," Mark grumbled, but the snort which followed put a lie to it.

"The knock on your head make you think you're funnier than before?"

Eric smiled at the familiarity of their banter. A month ago he would have listened to a couple more exchanges then called a halt to it, but now it sounded so good. But then, he could bring them back to earth. "Our lives are divided now, aren't they? Before the Accident. After the Accident. We'll use it to mark time."

"Jesus, Eric." Paulina drew back and tilted her head to look her husband in the eyes. "Aren't you off the drugs yet? And you *drove* out here?"

"You disagree?" *Just like him. Ignore the immediate question and dive further back in the conversation.*

"No." She drew out the word. "Not at all."

"Before the Accident, Pauli was…"

"Don't tax your mind, Mark." *Smart ass.* "Before the Accident I was a strong, successful woman." She shrugged. "After the Accident, I continue to be so." She raised an eyebrow at him. "Things don't have to change."

But they were going to. She had already determined that. Eric's accusation of her no longer being in love with him had rattled around in her brain for a week and finally landed in her soul where it had taken root. Yes, she still loved her husband. No, she wasn't still *in* love with him. But that didn't mean she wasn't going to try to be. Surely, that's what second chances were for, right?

"What was I thinking?" Mark exaggerated his tone. "Oh, I *was* thinking!"

Eric interrupted him. "I'm going to change. For the better."

"Now I know you're not off the drugs. You are too good already." How many times had they argued this very point? Eric was too good for his own--and the company's--good. Looked like some things wouldn't be changing because of the accident no matter what he thought.

"You think?"

"I know."

"How the hell are you going to change?" Mark pivoted toward them. He winced, and Paulina felt the now-familiar shot of guilt. She walked around virtually untouched while they struggled to move at all. Mark twisted his right leg, as if stretching his knee. Shouldn't he be in a wheelchair?

"I'm going to be nicer to my friends," Eric continued, oblivious to them. *Yes, still on drugs.*

"Crock of shit," Mark groused. *And maybe Mark should go back on them, the happy pill version.*

"You don't think I can be?"

"I'd like to know how you weren't nice in the first place."

"I told Sadie McCombs we were out of the azaleas

she wanted and planted roses instead. And still she killed them. How does anybody kill roses around here? I was just trying to save the poor azaleas."

Paulina snorted a laugh. "My God, Sadie McCombs. I never liked her. Hell, *you* never liked her. See, you don't have to be better for her."

"Just proving that I wasn't always nice."

"And Sadie McCombs died ten years ago."

"I bet Angel sent a pot of azaleas. That's her standard funeral thing. Azaleas."

"Fitting." Paulina summarized it for them. "So Sadie finally got them. What is the problem?"

"You're a piece of work, Pauli."

She chose to ignore him.

A car whizzed by, another, neither slowing down. They didn't turn to look, not even when one obnoxious horn blared and tires ground to a halt.

Who would dare disturb their peace, this reckoning? Everybody in four counties knew the story.

"So, you going to be nicer to them too?" Mark snarled. "Imposing on our quiet time?"

"Maybe. If they have a big front yard in need of serious landscaping."

Another long horn screech, followed by two short ones.

"Who's going to give in and look first?"

"Well, it won't be you, Pauli-girl."

"Is that my new nickname?"

"No, I'm still contemplating something with demolition in the title." He paused, and Paulina couldn't tell if the next words were choked out on laughter or pain. "Or deer."

Blare! *"Are you all deaf?"* Blare!

As one, they turned to see the Neely car parked behind their vehicles. Sarah Neely stood at the front grill, hands firmly planted on her hips. "I have a special delivery for you. Come fetch her!"

Seated sideways, one leg on the leather seat and the other left to dangle towards the floorboard in the back seat of Sarah Neely's car, Angel gave another involuntary shiver. Why didn't her ersatz chauffeur just walk over to the three of them? Why stand in front of the new Cadillac and scream? She drew a deep breath. Didn't she have better things to ponder? Surely, surely, she did.

Like how all four of them had survived. They shouldn't have. Someone should have died or been irreparably harmed. But, no, thanks to the mercy of God, all four would live to see Cancun another day. Not that she'd be wearing anything to the beach which revealed so much as an inch above her right knee. The car jolted from Sarah's slam of the trunk lid and Angel winced as she shifted her leg. One didn't slam a Caddy's trunk.

Sarah wrenched the door open, making Angel catch herself for balance. This was positively the last time she took Sarah up on her offer to take her anywhere she wanted to go. Not that her friend had been silent on Angel's choice of destination. Not at all.

"Now how are we going to do this?" Sarah asked. She set the brake on the wheelchair and tapped her foot. "Why I let you talk me into this fool..."

"Sarah, you are thrilled to be here. I know it and so do you."

"Angel, I'm just thrilled you can be here. And to show you how thrilled I am," she heaved a breath as she shoved the wheelchair until it collided with the car frame, "I'm going to leave you here for someone else to take home." She wedged her body between the chair and the open door. "Now grab the chair arms and scoot yourself back."

"I think there's an easier way to do this," she muttered as she started to comply.

"I think Paulina could get her ass over here."

"Paulina's ass is here." Angel and Sarah turned in the direction of Paulina's voice. "I'll take it from here, Sarah."

Angel felt her friend's sure hands under her arms and breathed easier as they maneuvered her into the chair.

"Good day, Sarah." Paulina dismissed her swiftly as she executed the chair into a sharp turn and headed toward their husbands.

Angel held onto the arms. "Thank you, Sarah," she called back as she watched Sarah climb behind the wheel. "Do you have to go so fast?" she asked over her shoulder and her voice rumbled on the gravel.

Paulina ignored her. "What are you doing out here?"

"I could ask you the same thing." Angel felt her temper rise as Mark half-turned and looked at her sheepishly. "Mark, you promised you were going to work and no where else."

"Look at Ms. I-just-want-to-stay-in-bed-all-day."

"I couldn't help it. Sarah came by and offered me a ride anywhere I wanted to go. *She* took pity on me."

Eric laughed deep in his throat and they turned to him. "The last time Angel wanted to stay in bed all day got her a kid."

"No, I promise you, Eric, it never took that long," Angel answered as Paulina halted their march.

"I am disparaged on every side. Don't you want to

get a shot in, Pauli?" Mark asked.

"Don't tempt me." She set the chair brake and returned to Eric's side.

"Since when did you need to be tempted?" Eric muttered just loudly enough for them all to hear.

Paulina opened her mouth to reply, but Angel cut her off. "You know, when I stop to think that I might never have heard all this good humor again..." Her voice broke and Mark limped the two steps to her side.

"Angel, angel, don't." He brushed away a tear on her cheek with his thumb. "Let's just be glad we're here."

"I am, Mark. Trust me, I am." She took his hand and splayed the fingers with her own. "It's just," she struggled for the words, "it's like after a storm, you know. When the last of the lightning is gone and the thunder has rolled away, then the birds come back out. You hear them chatter and you know it's all over. That the sun's about to shine." She squeezed their hands together. "I know there's so much yet to do to get back to normal... to *find* normal..."

"Shhh, Angel," Mark started, shaking his head.

"No, Mark." She looked up at him. "I hear the birds. I feel the sun."

"Oh, Ange." He pulled his hand from hers and smoothed the hair from her forehead. "I'd bend down and kiss you, but I'd never be able to straighten up without professional help."

"It's not a joke, Mark."

"I know that. I feel the sun, too."

Eric cleared his throat to break the tension. "Get a room."

"If your spouse hadn't taken my Jag off the cliff, I'd have one in Cancun about now."

"Yeah, well, I put my lawyer to work on that." He nudged Paulina with an elbow.

"And the resort promised to honor our reservations for a year. The airlines, I'm still working on."

"Poor airlines." Mark shook his head. "It's not even a contest."

"It just gives me longer to plot how to hide Paulina's bikini tops." Eric's voice was wistful.

"I thought you were going to start being good," she said.

"Sounds pretty good to me."

"This all just sounds pretty good to me," Angel sighed. "Don't worry, Paulina, you can have one of mine."

"No, thanks, sweetie. I don't think I can fill your cups."

"Enough!" Eric chuckled as he pulled on Paulina's arm and she helped him stand. "Let's finish this at home."

"Amen."

"Was that an 'amen' I heard from you, Pauli-girl?"

"No," she said, "that was a *grateful* amen."

About The Author

Kay Layton Sisk

Native Texan Kay Layton Sisk began writing books in third grade featuring such wonderful creatures as The Rainbow Monster. That opus may be hidden deep in the closet with the *Star Trek* fanfic she didn't know she was writing throughout high school. Then life took over and didn't release her to write again until staring at a computer screen resulted in more words than numbers.

Today she makes her home with one husband and seven demanding cats. Although she is the author of 12 romance novels, After the Thunder Rolls Away is her first foray into women's fiction. As with all the others, it began with "what if?"

You may follow her at
www.kaysisk.com,
kaysisk.blogspot.com (Sisker's Lair), or
kaylaytonsiskauthor on FaceBook.

Please watch for Kay Layton Sisk's next book,
Once Upon a McLeod